BONE DIGGER

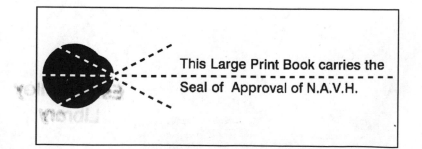

This Large Print Book carries the
Seal of Approval of N.A.V.H.

BONE DIGGER

DOUGLAS HIRT

WHEELER PUBLISHING
A part of Gale, Cengage Learning

GALE
CENGAGE Learning·

Farmington Hills, Mich • San Francisco • New York • Waterville, Maine
Meriden, Conn • Mason, Ohio • Chicago

LIBRARY OF CONGRESS CATALOGING-IN-PUBLICATION DATA

Hirt, Douglas.
  Bone digger / by Douglas Hirt. — Large print edition.
    pages cm. — (Wheeler Publishing large print western)
    ISBN 978-1-4104-8368-3 (softcover) — ISBN 1-4104-8368-1 (softcover)
    1. Ranches—Fiction. 2. Fossils—Fiction. 3. Paleontologists—Fiction.
  4. United States—Social life and customs—19th century—Fiction. 5. Large type books. I. Title.
  PS3558.I727B66 2015b
  813'.54—dc23   2015026162

Published in 2015 by arrangement with Hartline Literary Agency

Printed in the United States of America
1 2 3 4 5 6 7 19 18 17 16 15

BONE DIGGER

CHAPTER 1

The wind was like a telegraph wire that morning in October 1877, and Chad Larimer did not regard with favor the message it was sending his way. A scowl cracked his normally stony composure and cut furrows deep into his brow, above his narrowed gunmetal-gray eyes. C. L. McSween was a lot of things to a lot of men. He was both admired and hated, but there was one thing everyone agreed on — McSween was an honest man. That someone was stealing from him now cut Chad's fuse near the powder.

"What's the matter, Chad?" Eric looked up at him with those wide, searching eyes. The lad had a bright, curious mind, and Chad loved him as if he had been his own. Eric blinked in the sunlight. The big, floppy hat shading his eyes was four sizes too big for his head, but he wore it just the same — rain or blazes — even after Libby tucked him into his bed for the night. Well, the boy had his reasons, and it was going to take a mite more growing up on Eric Russman's part before he'd be able to bury them too.

But Eric was more grown-up than most folks gave him credit, and besides, it didn't take a bucket of brains to see that something was wrong. Maybe Chad had reined in too sharply at the first sign — even now his horse was protesting the bit in its mouth and pawing at the stiff, brown grass. He let up on the reins a bit and sniffed the wind again.

"Chad?"

If a man took stock of such things, Chad reckoned that there might be a hundred odors floating on the winds that swept along the high plains and rolled up against the eastern rise of the Rocky Mountains. A hundred different messages, some pleasant, others downright foul, such as riding upon a winter-kill cow festering out of a long freeze under a warm April sun. And then there were those peculiar smells that made a man instantly wary, that brought the hairs at the back of his neck ramrod straight.

"Chad–?"

The morning was warm for October, and too early for the wind to be moving around much. That was unfortunate, for had the breeze been stronger Chad might have been aware of them sooner. He glanced back at Eric's face, smooth and pink, and not yet ravaged by either time or the harshness of the open range.

"You stay here, Eric."

"But —"

"No buts." Chad swung off his horse and pulled his old Sharps .50 free of its saddle scabbard. He handed up the reins for Eric to hold and then added in a more gentle tone, "I don't want you gettin' hurt now, understand? Stay back here with the horses until I come back for you."

"Yes, sir." Eric frowned.

Being a kid was rough at times, but someday he would have his own stab at manhood, and Chad intended to make sure nothing happened to the boy to prevent it. He gave Eric a long look. It wasn't like Eric to give in so easily. "I'll be back soon, son."

He crouched swiftly through the stiff grass that whispered past his legs, making for a ravine that lay a couple hundred paces to the west. Just shy of the rim, he dropped and bellied up to the lip Comanche-style, pushing his rifle ahead of him. As he neared it, the smell grew into a bitter stench carried on the upwelling draft. Now Chad identified another odor as well. Smoke from a piñon wood fire.

Chad pushed up the last few feet to the edge of the ravine. It was something called protein in the flesh and hair that made such a foul stink when burned, he recalled someone telling him once in the branding pens. He whipped off his hat and poked a cautious eye over the rim.

Three men were down there, two whites and a long-haired, coal-eyed Indian. The Indian's hands were full with a struggling cow — McSween's cow! He'd wrestled the animal to the ground while one of the whites put muscle and sweat into a taunt trip-rope looped about the animal's kicking hind legs. The third fellow lifted a glowing running iron from a bed of red coals and moved over the cow.

Smoke curled into the air, the cow bellowed, and the fellow putting his weight onto the trip-rope glanced around nervously. Chad didn't recognize them. They were not any of the local folks that he knew of. He figured them for a small outfit passing through and getting a herd together the easy way.

Chad glanced down the ravine where five cows were huddled together in a rope corral strung up between three cottonwood trees. Below, a stream trickled softly and there a seventh animal stood tied to a tree, waiting its turn at the iron. Chad studied it some. These hombres must have been running late. He guessed they had expected to have the stealing done before sunrise, but something must have happened to delay them, and now the sun was already an hour off the horizon. The fellow with the rope didn't appear to like the daylight. Men like him usually don't.

He backed away from the edge of the ravine and when he turned around Eric was standing right there, the reins in his fingers, the horses tugging at the brown tuffs of dry buffalo grass, and a look of intrigue in his wide eyes.

"I told you to stay put!" he whispered, anger in his voice.

"What —"

He grabbed Eric by the arm and hauled him away. He didn't stop until they were safely down in a hollow.

"What's down there, Chad?" Eric asked as Chad sat him unceremoniously upon the ground.

"The next time I tell you to stay put, you stay! Lord knows, you will get your blame fool head blown off if'n you don't listen to me! And mine too!" Chad drew in a long breath. Eric's eyes grew misty.

11

Chad let go of his anger. "Don't take it to heart, Eric. I can't fault you for being curious. Shoot, when I was a tadpole your age I was curious as an antelope myself. Only, I didn't have no one to look out for me."

"I'm sorry, Chad. I didn't mean no harm."

"I know, son. I just couldn't bear having you get hurt."

"What's going on down there, Chad?" His voice was excited.

"Some yahoos stealing your grandpa's beeves, and I reckon it's my job to put a stop to it."

"Rustlers?"

"Three of 'em with a running iron and getting nervous."

"What are we going to do about it, Chad?"

Chad frowned. "*We* aren't going to do anything about it. *You* are going to stay right here in this old buffalo wallow and keep your head down. Me, I've a mind of what I'm going to do, but you'll have no piece of it."

The gleam in Eric's face dimmed a bit, but he understood this was dangerous business. "Yes, sir."

Chad checked the load in the chamber of his Sharps and made his way back to the rim, skirting the ravine as he moved along it until the declivity made a sharp bend that put him out of sight of the men below. Quietly he slipped down the sandy slope toward the trickle of water at its bottom.

It had been a drought summer with little rainfall, and so far there had been no snowfall in the mountains to the west. In past years Chad had known this stream to run belly deep to a tall horse, but not this year. The parched ground and dry winds had sapped its moisture, and the hard summer had killed many of McSween's cows — had stolen them just as surely as these three were stealing them now. Chad had felt helpless watching good beef stagger and die under a hellish sun for lack of water, but he had no such sympathy when it came to dealing with cattle thieves.

There was no cover down by the water as Chad worked his way back to where the thieves had set up their branding operation, but the rustlers were busy hauling down a thrashing cow, not expecting anyone to be creeping up on them. Chad halted just beyond the rope corral, behind an ancient cottonwood, and put the heavy Sharps rifle to his shoulder as the rustlers were about to press the glowing iron over C. L. McSween's Rocking S brand.

"Hold it right there!"

The three came about at once, startled.

13

"Let go of that beef and back away."

The cow kicked to its feet, shucking the trip-rope and scrambled up the embankment.

"Now, unbuckle those gun belts and let 'em drop." He moved more away from the tree.

"How 'bout we talk about this, mister," the man holding the running iron said.

"Your gun belts. On the ground. Now!" Chad centered his sights on the big fellow's chest and quietly prayed they wouldn't reach for their revolvers. He had no desire to kill anyone, but kill he would if they made a move for their guns.

The Indian had frozen like a cigar-store statue, but the nervous one, the fellow with the slack end of the trip-rope still in his grasp, didn't like the notion of Chad taking him in. His hand wavered a moment, his eyes narrowing.

Chad had a sudden feeling of helplessness, as if the situation was swiftly going to get out of hand.

The man dropped the rope and his hand stabbed at the revolver at his side. In a heartbeat, his revolver cleared leather.

The big Sharps roared. The man a dozen paces away cartwheeled backwards, sprawled in the dust near the stream, and did not move.

The other two men watched in stunned silence. Chad drew his revolver and laid the rifle on the ground, not taking his eyes off of them.

"You . . . you killed him," the white man said. He didn't need any further prodding and fumbled at the buckle of his gun belt and let it fall. The Indian was armed only with a long-bladed knife that he tossed alongside the holster.

Chad's heart was racing as he stepped forward and grabbed up the trip-rope, and the knife. He took a long breath then cut a length of rope and tossed it to the Indian. "Tie his hands behind him, and make sure you do it right."

His black eyes locked onto Chad, then slowly he turned toward the white man and tied his wrists behind him. Chad threw a loop around the Indian's wrists, snugged it down and tied it off.

"On the ground. Pronto."

They lowered themselves onto their bellies. The white man tilted up his head. "Hey, mister, you let us go we'll not say a word about you killin' Frank. Let's make a deal?"

Chad glanced along the ravine and found their horses tied to a leaning cottonwood tree down by the water.

"I got me some money, mister," he continued. "You can have it all if you let me and the Chief go."

"This here is Rocking S land, and them's Rocking S cows, and they both belong to C. L. McSween." Chad recovered his rifle from the ground and breaking the action, ejected a long, brass cartridge. He slipped a fresh round into the breech and closed the block. "The way I see it, it's Mr. McSween you need to deal with, not me."

"You turn us over to this McSween fellow and he's likely to string us up?"

"That is likely," Chad agreed.

The white man had begun to sweat, but the Indian remained unmoved, black eyes burning with hate.

"I've heard about McSween. He's a hard man. How about you take us into the sheriff at Cañon City instead?"

"What makes you think a judge won't make you swing? A man with a hot running iron and standing over McSween cattle is evidence enough for any jury. Anyway, this is McSween's land, and on it he's law." Chad looked at the body of the man called Frank. A pool of thickening red had spread out on the dirt beneath him. A pang of regret squeezed his chest. He'd killed before, and in the world he lived in, he'd

16

probably have to kill again, but that didn't make it rest any easier on his spirit. He was still numbed by the rush of the encounter. Later, when his blood settled, then he'd feel it — the regret, the questions.

Thou shall not kill.

Which commandment was that? The sixth? Seventh? He could never keep them straight, even though Parson Greenbrake had preached on the matter more than once. Just the same, he knew this wasn't exactly what the Lord had in mind when he spoke of killing. This was self-defense killing, not out-and-out murder killing. And didn't the Lord somewhere tell his apostles to sell their cloak and buy a sword? That surely was for self-defense. Well, he could talk his way around the matter a dozen different ways, but the plain fact of it was killing left a bitter, empty feeling in him, and a churning in his stomach.

"Leastwise, you two are better off than your friend over there."

The man's eyes lingered upon the dead man a moment, then turned back with the fire of fear burning behind them. "Listen, mister. I've got me forty dollars in my saddlebags. It's all yours if you just let me go. You can keep the Chief."

The Indian's view shifted and locked upon

the other man. Chad thought he caught a glint of humor in the stoic face.

"I guess you must be hard of hearing."

"What good will turning us in do you? On the other hand, forty dollars can buy a lot of forgetting, mister." He was sweating hard, and with good reason. Cattle stealing was not looked lightly upon in this land. Even being caught with a running iron lashed to your saddle was provocation enough for some folks to reach for the nearest rope. Being caught red-handed was sure enough a ticket to the nearest tree.

"The kind of forgetting you're talking about, the kind that money buys, makes for mighty poor sleeping at night, friend." Chad nodded toward the cows. "Good beef was bringing fourteen dollars a head the last I heard. Seems to me that if you are offering to buy those cows now, you're about eighty dollars shy of the asking price. Maybe McSween will sell them to you, and maybe not. He might consider that forty dollars of yours a down payment, but I wouldn't count on it. Knowing Mr. McSween, he'd sooner make you eat that money than sell his beeves to the likes of you. But that isn't my decision."

Chad brought their horses up, lifted the dead man onto his saddle, lashing feet and hands together under the animal's belly. He made two loops in what remained of the trip-rope, about twenty feet apart, and dropped one over each man's head, cinching them down.

"Mount up."

Chad helped the white man climb into his saddle, but the Indian did not move.

Chad lifted his rifle. "You can ride on your saddle, or tied across it. The choice is yours and I don't much care which way you want it, only you best decide soon. I'm about run out of patience."

His black eyes burned with the fires of hell itself, but he wasn't ready to die today. He grabbed the saddle horn with his bound hands and swung up on the horse.

Chad wrapped the end of the tether around the dead man's saddle horn and taking up its reins, started the animals out of the ravine. The metallic clack of a Winchester rifle levering a shell into the chamber stopped him, his blood turning to ice. On the rim above sat a big man astride a stout bay horse.

The man must have lost his hat somewhere back along the trail for the morning sun gleamed off his bald head. A slow smile hitched up the corner of his mouth, and in his right hand he held a short barrel '73.

But that wasn't what made Chad's heart beat faster. What made Chad grow sick inside was what his left arm held — a squirming little boy wearing a hat four sizes too large.

CHAPTER 2

"Woolf!" the white man blurted out with sudden relief. "Thank God you came back in time."

"Heard a shot." Woolf glanced at the body tied across the saddle. "I see Frank got it. Well, I ain't surprised. He worried most about someone finding us out. Turned back on my trail and run across this here whelp tending two horses down a wallows. It didn't take much figuring to know what'd happened."

"Let the boy go," Chad said.

The man looked at him. "Well, now, it seems to me that this here kid is our safe ticket out of here . . . what do you think, Bill? How 'bout you, Chief?"

The Indian remained silent, not even his eyes revealing what he was thinking.

"I'll hold onto the kid a while longer, and in the meantime you best untie my friends and not be slow about it."

21

Chad's choices were few at the moment, but so long as he still had Woolf's friends in ropes, he had something to bargain with. He weighed the matter. Woolf might tag him with that rifle, shooting one-handed like he'd have to, but there was no way 'round the plain fact that no matter what Chad tried, the first blood spilled would be Eric's.

"What will it be, mister? You loose my friends, or do I start carving up the kid?"

Chad drew in a breath. "All right. I'll do as you say . . ."

Whomph! The report of a heavy rifle came from somewhere nearby and Woolf's skull parted above his eyebrows . . . His strings cut, Woolf toppled from the saddle taking Eric with him.

Chad wheeled about in time to see the distant rider lowering a rifle from his shoulder.

Eric had picked himself off the ground by time Chad scrambled up out of the ravine. Eric was sobbing and Chad took the boy in his arms. His skin was ghost-white, and blood had splattered down the front of his shirt.

"Are you all right, Eric?"

"I . . . I'm all right, I think, Chad."

Chad hugged him tight, and then looked across the ravine as the rider rode down the long slope of the hill beyond. The man on the horse was tall under a broad hat. He reined to a halt on the other side of the ravine and casually rested the butt of a long-barreled rifle upon his thigh. The rifle was peculiar for the glinting attachment upon the barrel. Chad was too far off to be certain, but it appeared be a long, brass tube. A telescopic sight? He'd heard of such things but had never seen one.

The rider looked down inside the ravine at the two prisoners, then shouted across it, "It does appear that you have your hands full, mister."

"Seems that way." The man had the look of a wrangler, but he seemed to sit a bit stiff in the saddle. He may or may not have been a wrangler, but as far as Chad could remember, he never did know any cowboy who could shoot worth a darn — except at rattlesnakes or coyotes — and then they seldom hit those unless they were right on top of them.

"Is the boy all right?"

Color was beginning to flood back into Eric's cheeks, and he was fidgeting, wanting to be let loose of. Chad nodded his head. "He's fine. This button has got the bravado of a tomcat." He thought he saw a grin spread the stranger's face, but couldn't be sure. The wide hat shaded most of his face, and all that Chad was sure of was that whoever this stranger was, he was one crackerjack marksman! A knot of anger bloomed in his chest and Chad didn't know what it was about.

Chad took Eric away from the body and knelt down, bringing his eyes level with the boy's. "You okay?"

"I'm still a little shaky, Chad. A little scared, I think."

He gave him a smile and another hug. "Any man who had gone through what you just did would be a little scared. You did just fine, Eric. Handled yourself like a real man."

Eric's eyes brightened. They were brown eyes, like his pa's had been; brown as polished walnuts while his mother's eyes were bluer than a mountain lake.

"Really?"

"I wouldn't green you 'bout something like that. Your pa would have been peacock-proud of you. Handled yourself like I've seen him do a time or two."

Eric's smile grew into the biggest grin Chad had ever seen, and he figured he'd said enough. Chad usually held back his feelings about Gary Russman, never much caring to tell a lie — or have to. When you are a nine-year-old boy you're still too young to bear the truth of some things, particularly when those things are about the only man you'd ever loved and honored — your father. Chad had stretched the truth from time to time when speaking to Eric about his father, but he had never lied to the boy. He could never abide by the story Libby had told Eric about how Gary Russman had died. When pressed to add a word, Chad would just grunt and say, "Whal, I wasn't there when it happened, son." He hoped Eric would understand and not be too awful bitter the day the truth finally did come out.

"Here comes that stranger," Eric said, pointing across the ravine. The man had started down the loose, sandy slope, allowing his horse to pick its own way down.

"I'd better find out who this *sharpshooter* is. Think you can find our horses?"

"Sure thing!" Eric was up like a shot. He stopped then, suddenly, and looked back at him. "I stayed put this time, Chad, just like you told me to do."

"I know, son."

That pleased the boy, and he was off like nothing had ever happened. *The bravado of a tomcat,* Chad reflected, holding back a grin. Then he went back down into the ravine where his prisoners were still tied. Something was eating at him and he suddenly realized what it was.

The stranger reined in, studied Chad a moment, then the two men in the rope. An easy smile moved across his face and when he swung out of his saddle and was standing firm on his own two feet, Chad moved toward him and shot out a fist. It smacked his chin with a crack and the man stumbled backwards, his rifle flying. He lay there a moment, stunned, then he managed to sit up. He wiped the blood from his mouth, his eyes wide and confused.

"Did I plug the wrong fellow?"

"What did you think you were doing? Shooting aces in a circus sideshow," Chad barked, standing over him. "If your bullet had flown six inches lower I'd be burying the boy as well."

The man laughed, then winced and worked his jaw experimentally. "Is that all?"

"Is that all?"

He started to get up, then reconsidered, evidently deciding it was safer to remain where he was — at least until the introductions were out of the way.

"If I had thought for one instant I couldn't hit what I was aiming at, I wouldn't have pulled the trigger. From where I was sitting up on that ridge, watching it through the glass, it appeared that man had you and the kid wedged between the proverbial rock and hard place."

Chad studied him. He didn't ride like a cowboy, and he sure didn't talk like any he'd met before, but he had to admit the truth of what he said. "We were. I couldn't bear to lose that boy, and I'm obliged that you came along when you did, mister."

The man grinned and rubbed his jaw. "I am certainly pleased to hear that, because I think I'd regret running into you if you were really upset at me."

Chad offered him a hand up. "My name is Chadwick Larimer, but my friends just call me Chad — at least to my face."

"Alexander Stovill the Second — but my friends call me Alex . . ." His fist came up catching Chad beneath the ribs and staggering him back against the Indian's horse. Chad sat hard upon the ground, fighting to draw in a breath.

Stovill was grinning.

"It is a pleasure to meet you, Alex," Chad said when he could draw a breath.

Stovill helped him up. "Pleasure's all mine, Chad."

Chad held his gut and gave a groan as he came to his feet. "I know an old mule that kicks about like you punch. Where are you from? Where you bound?"

"I'm down from Denver City."

"You know you are on Rocking S land?"

"I certainly hope I am. Otherwise that fellow in Cañon City who gave me the directions was sending me on a fool's ride."

"You have business here?"

"Of sorts." Stovill retrieved his rifle from the dirt, brushed the dust from the long, brass tube along its barrel, and blew into the lens. "I heard that Mr. McSween might be hiring on some more hands. You work for Mr. McSween, Chad?"

"I'm his foreman, and Eric there is his grandson. I don't know where you heard we was hiring."

"Some fellow in Cañon City."

"Who?"

"Didn't bother to ask his name."

"Then he knows something I don't," Chad said. "Unless he was thinking about the dam."

"Dam?"

"Mr. McSween is building it up Thunder Canyon. He might have put out word for more laborers, but I haven't heard of it."

"I think I am beginning to look pretty foolish."

"Whal, never mind that. Come along with

me to the house and see what Mr. McSween has to say about it. At least we can fill your stomach with some of Cookie's good grub before you head back to Cañon City or Denver."

"That is fair enough."

Chad glanced at Woolf's body on the rim of the ravine. "Help me load that big one across his saddle." He gathered the reins of the three horses.

"Hey, Mr. Stovill," Bill called, turning in his saddle. "I got me forty dollars. It's yours if you get us out of here. No one will know."

Stovill inclined his head toward Chad. "He'll know, and he might have something to say about that."

The tortured look on the man's face said clearly that he wanted Stovill to use that rifle one more time. Chad said, "Sounds to me like you've just been made a cash offer, Alex."

"It sort of sounded that way to me too. But my gun isn't for hire."

It was a matter-of-fact statement, but at that instant spider legs crawled up Chad's spine. He gave a small shiver and drew in a breath. It had been one of those mornings, and it was going to take some time for his nerves to ease back off their hair-trigger setting.

Then Eric appeared on the rim of the ravine.

"Got the horses, Chad," he said, waving.

They mounted up and headed back to the headquarters.

CHAPTER 3

Clarence Leroy McSween filled the doorway of the long, low house like a hungry grizzly bear, his fierce eyes two chunks of blue ice stabbing out from the wild reddish-brown mane that encircled his chin and engulfed his broad head. Those eyes watched them now as they rode under the Rocking S shingle that swayed in the slight breeze. Chad took note of that glare in his boss's eyes as he led the train of horses laden with their cargo of dead and bound into the yard and up the lane that circled around to the front of the house.

McSween stepped out onto the covered porch that stretched the length of the house, and down the three stone steps to meet them. He moved with the fluid motion of a cat stalking prey; a certain easiness of limb and shoulder that seemed out of place in a man weighing well over two hundred seventy pounds. McSween had the height to distribute all that weight, and his feline grace came from an earlier life spent in Indian country trapping beaver, and then later hunting buffalo. He'd taken up raising beef fifteen years previously — just after those first hostile shots fired in April of '61 when some South Carolinians at Charleston Harbor decided the federal troops should be made to leave Southern land one way or the other. McSween had missed out on that conflict, content instead to fight the Arapaho that ranged along the eastern rise of the Rocky Mountains.

It had been a long road for McSween; one begun as an aspiring Harvard Law professor and ending here, on the windswept Colorado prairie. The years had done their work well, fairly scouring C. L. McSween of all traces of that tamer past in a world grown too fat, too civilized, and too regimented for his liking . . . at least on the surface.

McSween waited for Chad to draw up. In a glance he took in the five strangers — two dead and three still alive. His view narrowed toward the running iron tied to the saddle of one of the dead men. His eyes shifted to Eric's tight-lipped face, back to Chad's hooded scowl, then to Stovill and the rifle he held across his knees.

He frowned. "Those big buffalo guns sure do make a mess."

Stovill said, "A man hit with one rarely gets up and walks away."

McSween grunted his understanding then looked at Eric. "You feeling all right, boy?"

"Yes, Grandpa."

"That's not fully the truth, but I'll let it pass this time. You're looking a mite ashen, Eric. Run on inside and find your ma. She'll be the devil to live with once she gets an eyeful of this."

"Yes, sir." Eric climbed off his horse and ran inside.

A couple wranglers from the bunkhouse started over.

McSween looked at the dead men. "Who're these, Chad?"

"I caught them with a hot iron and some of your cows down along Coal Creek."

"I see." His brow furrowed. "We've been fortunate. It's been a while since we had to deal with cow thieves, but the problem never seems to go away. If it isn't the Arapaho, it's yahoos like these. And him?" McSween's view pounced upon Stovill.

"He happened to be in a handy place when I needed a hand."

"Bristol." McSween called one of the wranglers over.

"Yes, sir, Mr. McSween?" Bristol was a tall, leather-faced man beneath a weather-beaten Stetson hat.

"Haul these two off somewhere before they ripen up on us. Then take the ones still breathing around back." McSween squinted up at the sun, hot in the thin air. "Set them down in the shade and give them some water. Tend to the horses too while you're at it."

"Right, boss." Bristol hooked an arm at another man and the two of them led the horses away.

McSween said, "Come inside, Chad. Tell me what happened. You too, Mr. — ?"

"Stovill, sir. Alexander Stovill the Second, but my friends just call me Alex."

"Hum." McSween considered him a moment as a wolf might a lone sheep. "Well, you come along too, *Mister* Stovill." He strove back up the steps like a locomotive gathering steam.

"McSween! I got me forty dollars. It's yours if you let me go," Bill called back as Bristol was leading his horse away.

McSween wheeled about on the porch and considered the man a moment.

Chad said, "That money is burning a hole in his pocket. He's been trying to give it away ever since I caught him."

"Is that so?"

Bill's face was streaming sweat, his eyes widened by fear.

McSween said, "The way I see it, once we put a rope around your neck, that money will be mine anyway. Just the same, I don't reckon I need your forty dollars, and I wouldn't take it in exchange for a cow thief's neck if I was cash broke and up to my beard in debt. But I'll tell you what I will do. I'll take that money and hand it over to the constable at Cañon City to pay for the four burials he's gonna have on his hands. That's only fair, don't you think? No reason the hardworking folk of Cañon should have to pick up the bill for planting you."

"You're a heartless sonofa—"

Bristol yanked his horse forward and Bill nearly lost his saddle. He struggled to regain it as Bristol led him away.

McSween grinned. "Ain't that the truth of the matter," he said under his breath and went inside the house.

Chad fidgeted in the thick, leather chair. He'd never been content to sit in one place for very long, and now his muscles fairly screamed to be released from their confinement and his long legs yearned to stretch

— preferably across the back of his horse. Astride a good working animal was the one place Chad could remain for hours on end — anyplace else soon became torture. Here, in McSween's office, Chad was doubly confined.

The room was small to begin with, and McSween huge, with a commanding oak desk sized to fit its owner. Upon its scuffed top lay open a thick ledger book that McSween likely had been writing in a few minutes before they arrived. The combination of that and the five people there was claustrophobic, but what really made Chad's skin crawl was not the tightness of the place but the books! A solid wall of them! Shelves and shelves of leather-bound and clothbound books. The messages hidden in the letters and words were as much a mystery to him as the inside workings of the big locomotives that rumbled along the new rails that the Santa Fe Railroad had put down not too many miles east of the Rocking S.

A good horse and a cow to work, and none could best him. But put a book in his hands and the world started crashing in. Reading had never played a large part in Chad's life. He knew enough about letters and his ciphers to do his job, and for years that was all he figured he needed to know. It wasn't that he did not want to learn to read, it is just that somehow, over the course of his life, no one had bothered to teach him how. His mother had died young, and his grandfather had been as helpless with words as he. Chad had heard some of the stories, of course, and he knew vast horizons were locked between those cloth and leather covers that no cow pony could ever cross — and for that reason he mostly avoided Mc-Sween's little office except when he had to be there. Like now.

"That is dreadful!" Libby said, giving Eric's shoulder a squeeze that made the boy wince and twist out of her grasp. Her face had twisted from fear to horror when Chad had told them the events of that morning, and now she grabbed her son in a death grip that threatened she might never let him out of her sight again.

That is just what the boy doesn't need now.

"Yes, ma'am, it certainly was," Stovill said, and Chad could see in his eyes that Stovill was fascinated by her — as are most men the first time they lay eyes upon Libby Mc-Sween Russman.

"You are a Godsend, Mr. Stovill. I tremble to think what might have happened to Eric if *you* had not arrived when you did." Her view shot accusingly at Chad, and the overstuffed chair where he sat was suddenly unbearable — if that was any more possible.

Hadn't he promised her he'd take care of her son? Didn't he profess great affection for the boy — and for his mother too? Well, it wasn't as though he went out of his way to put Eric in jeopardy. He could have sent the boy hightailing it back to his mama's apron strings at the first whiff of danger.

More apron strings! Chad thought bitterly. Ever since that night his father died, Libby had had Eric cinched in tighter than a bone corset.

McSween cleared his throat, and the desk chair creaked as he rocked back in it. "There are two things I value the most in this world, Mr. Stovill." His words drew Libby's fiery glare off of Chad. "My family" — McSween's eyes shifted, taking in Libby and Eric, then back at Stovill — "and this ranch. The way I see it, you did right by me on both accounts this morning, and I am in your debt."

Stovill seemed lost for words. McSween went on before he could find them. "Chad tells me you were on Rocking S land looking for a job."

"Yes, sir. It was said you might be hiring."

"We might. We're full up far as wranglers

go, but we always can use a stout back and strong arms for that project down at Thunder Canyon. What do you think, Chad?"

"I can vouch for his strong arm." He put a hand to his stomach. "And a hard fist."

"Are you opposed to hard work, Mr. Stovill? Most wranglers despise any task that can't be done on the back of a horse."

"No, sir, Mr. McSween. Hard work never bothered me."

"It'll be temporary, but it will see you through the winter. If you work out, come spring maybe you can move in permanent, that is, if you still have a mind to work for me." McSween grinned. "After you get to know us better, you might have different ideas."

"That sounds more than fair, sir."

"Good." McSween looked at Chad. "Now that's settled, what are we going to do with that Indian and his partner with the forty dollars?"

"That's up to you. It was your beeves they was stealing."

"Ten years ago I'd have strung 'em up behind the barn." McSween's eyes narrowed. "What are you grinning at?"

"You're going soft, C. L."

"I prefer to think of it as mellowing." McSween smiled and leaned back in his chair.

"When Libby's mother was alive, she fancied this massive family Bible. It was thick as my arm and weighed enough to moor a schooner at anchor during a gale. An awesome book it was, and Millicent used to haul it around with her and read aloud from it whenever she happened upon a passage she figured the Lord meant for my ears. One of the more frequent ones I recall was, *Vengeance is mine, saith the Lord.*"

He thought a moment, a shine coming to his eyes. "I'm not a young man and someday I'll be in Mr. Stovill's shoes, only it will be the Almighty's door I'll be knocking on, asking for a job. I don't particularly want his foreman to turn this old cowhand away because once I ride that trail, Chad, there are only two outfits left to work for, and frankly, I never much liked the heat." He laughed. "Soft, am I? I say it's giving back to the Lord a little of the authority I took, which never did belong to me in the first place.

"Have a couple of the boys take those two yahoos into Cañon City this afternoon and turn them over to the constable there. They'll most likely end up stretching a rope, but it won't be by my hand."

McSween pushed back from the desk and stood. "Take Mr. Stovill to the bunkhouse and get him settled in. Then tell Bristol I want to talk to him."

"Father," Libby interrupted, "perhaps Mr. Stovill would join us for dinner tonight?"

Chad looked up with a start. Rarely did hired hands eat at McSween's table. C. L. seemed surprised by the request too, but upon thinking it over said, "How about it, Stovill? You'll be enduring Cookie's grub soon enough."

"I'd like that very much, Mr. McSween." His eyes remained on Libby longer than Chad thought was proper for a first acquaintance and a small knot of tension tightened in his chest.

Libby McSween Russman stood tall and straight, with the bearing of a woman of means and influence. Beside that, she was prettier than a whole mountain glade of columbine. That beauty had charmed some of the finest Eastern schools. McSween had seen to it that Libby's shoulders had managed to brush against people of influence, and when she returned to Colorado, the Territory was not nearly wide enough to contain all that newly acquired prestige.

But that was back when she'd been but a young woman. The years had not been so kind, rubbing some of the gleam off her Eastern polish. A son brought her highfalutin ways back to earth and a husband's indiscretions had trampled her pride into the mud. But like the stubborn cactus rose, when her long winter finally came to spring, she bloomed. True, her world had shriveled from the highlife of Boston and New York down to a few hundred square miles of prairie and cactus, but it was her haven now — or was it a prison? Chad had not yet made up his mind on that.

Libby said, "We eat at six thirty. I'll have Rosita serve up something special." With a flourish of blue gingham she turned and hurried Eric out of the office.

There was a long moment of silence, as if Libby's presence had been the only reason for them being there, and now that reason was gone.

Chad spoke first. "Come with me, Stovill. I'll introduce you around." He plucked his hat off the side table and left.

CHAPTER 4

The wagon rolled away under the Rocking S shingle and turned into the fading sunlight. The best Chad could arrange on short notice was a couple blankets spread over them, but the trip into Cañon City was only twenty miles and the evening was already turning cool. They'd keep till morning.

Bill and the Apache rode their own horses tied to the back of the wagon. Chad had made certain their knots were fixed right and that they'd not work their hands loose during the journey.

"You look worried." Libby's words half startled him. He'd not heard her walking up behind him. She stood at his side, her hands folded in front of her, no longer wearing gingham but a gray riding skirt and pale-blue shirtwaist. Her long yellow hair was pulled back and held in a pale-blue ribbon. Her eyes, the color of columbine flowers, caught the lowering sunlight. Libby's

43

beauty would always be his weak spot. He longed to take her in his arms right now. But this was neither the time nor the place.

"What makes you think I'm worried?"

"I can tell."

He gazed into her searching eyes then nodded at the wagon with its cargo of dead men. "Not to worry, Libby. Just thinking. It's men like that, who bring trouble into life. What would this land be like if they weren't here?"

"Like a garden, but that was lost a long time ago."

He gave a short laugh. "Reckon I keep forgetting about that."

She smiled and shivered in the evening chill, hugging her arms about her waist. "I'm sorry . . . about this morning. I know you wouldn't do anything to harm Eric."

He felt his lips tighten and forced them to relax. "I know, Libby."

"Do you?"

How could a man ever know the feeling of a mother toward her child? That sort of protectiveness was instinctive in all mothers, human and animal. "I don't have to tell you how I feel about Eric."

She touched his arm. "You've been like a father to him — better than his real father."

His throat tightened. The question was,

would he ever be more? Would Libby ever let him that far into her life? How could she when he could barely write his own name. She lived in a different world from his. Her expectations were too lofty for an un-schooled cowboy to ever reach. He cleared his throat. "If you're to be a proper hostess tonight, shouldn't you be getting all fancied up?"

"Fancied up? What on earth for? There's only going to be you and Father, and that Stovill fellow — what's his name?"

"His name is Alex, and you know that as good as me."

Libby laughed. "Are you trying to be shed of little ol' me?" she teased.

"I'd be a blame fool to try that. I may not be book-learned, but I'm not crazy."

She drew in a long breath and let it out. "Well, you are not crazy, and you are right. I should be getting ready. I need to check in on Rosita, anyway. See you at dinner."

Chad nodded.

"Take me for a moonlight stroll after-ward?"

"That would be my pleasure."

"Till then." Her lashes fluttered and she gazed longingly and playfully at the sky and patted her hand rapidly over her heart. He laughed. At one time Libby had entertained thoughts of the stage. Nothing ever came of it, but there lingered a bit of the thespian in her soul.

McSween brought his huge paw down hard on the table, rattling the plates. "Rosita!" he bellowed glaring at the kitchen door.

"Si, señor?" answered a small voice. Rosita appeared in the doorway, unsure whether it was safe to venture into the dining room.

"How often do I have to remind you? Knife and spoons on the right, forks on the left. I don't mind you mixing them up when it's just Libby and me, but when we have company, I expect you to conform to formal standards of etiquette!" He snorted and said to Stovill, "I try to bring a little culture to the wilderness and no one seems to care."

"I care, Father."

His scowl melted. "My ray of sunshine. Thank you, my dear."

"Pardon me for saying so, Mr. McSween, but I hardly would have expected you to appreciate the finer details of life?"

"Is that a fact?" His ice-blue eyes scrutinized Stovill. "Let me tell you something. When I was your age the East started crowding the south side of my chin. Life in Cambridge was about as confining as living in a corset."

"Father, please."

"Sorry, dear, but that's how it felt. Sort of like the back of a spiny horse, if you get my drift, Stovill."

"I do," he said grinning.

"So I fled for the wide fresh spaces of the West, leaving the place to the dandies and the fine ladies who didn't seem to mind living in hobbles. I spent well over half my life in the mountains. Trapped the beaver until the fur trade dried up. Afterward, I hunted game for the railroad and fought my share of Indians and claim jumpers. But the writing was on the wall and I wasn't getting any younger so I cut this here ranch out of a wilderness and married a fine woman and had me a fine daughter." He paused and became introspective.

"I haven't been back to Cambridge in over forty years. I don't miss the anthill one whit. But just because the East smothers a man, surely as fingers about his throat, does not mean I reject culture and the advances man has achieved. A man needs to keep his feet in the present and his eyes to the future or he will find himself too deeply mired in the past to be of any earthly good to anyone."

"I see you are a philosopher as well, Mr. McSween. I couldn't agree with you more.

This is the very reason I find myself out west."

McSween contemplated the younger man like a wolf studying a chicken in the center of a snare. "You don't talk like any wrangler I ever did meet."

"And neither do you, I dare say." Stovill smiled easily. "Just how is a wrangler supposed to speak? I'm afraid I lost most of my sand at Yale, class of seventy-two."

"Yale!" McSween perked up. "I'm a Harvard man, myself."

"That's a mighty shame," Stovill said and the two of them laughed as though he had made a joke, and carried on like long-lost school chums. Chad kept silent, feeling like a clay pot in a china cabinet. All he knew about Harvard and Yale was that they were fancy places a man went off to, to get his head filled with book learning. He couldn't be bothered by it, but what did bother him was the way Libby's eyes seemed to shine whenever they fell upon Stovill, and Chad was aware they settled there often now.

Rosita brought in the food and set it around. Dinner conversation included little else than talk of the East and their schools, and by the time dinner was finished Chad was as edgy as a barefooted man in a cactus patch. Worse even than sitting in McSween's

48

office staring at all those silent books. He was about to excuse himself when McSween changed subjects.

"Chad, tomorrow I want you to ride into Thunder Canyon and start rounding up any of our cows that might have roamed up the stream." McSween pushed back his plate, wiped his lips and signaled for Rosita to bring him his humidor. He passed out cigars to each of them and when he got his burning to his satisfaction said, "Harrison and Timbledee tell me the first level of the dam should be completed within the month. I want to start filling it immediately and don't want any animals trapped back in there once we begin. Think you'll need any help?"

Chad shook his head. "The men will be better used building the dam. Likely won't be more'n two or three strays up there anyway." He pulled on the sweet Cuban cigar.

Libby stood. "If you all will excuse me, I'll busy myself elsewhere while you three talk. Eric, come along."

Stovill rose to his feet and Chad was suddenly uncomfortable. He knew it was proper to stand when a lady entered or left a room, but this was Libby. Just the same, Stovill had taken the lead, and Chad felt compelled to follow. He awkwardly half stood then sat back in his chair. There was an amused glint in McSween's eyes as he remained seated, watching, studying both of them. After Libby and Eric left the room Stovill sat and flashed a smile at Chad. Chad suspected it was a victory signal of some sort and that victories probably came easily to Alexander Stovill.

McSween cleared his throat, rousing their attention again. "As for you, Stovill, hauling dirt on a digging crew is backbreaking work. Any cowman worth his spurs would despise the job."

"It won't bother me, sir."

"Hum." McSween chewed the end of his cigar. "Somehow I didn't figure it would. Last summer we went five months without rain. The hottest year anyone hereabouts can recall, including the Arapaho. Lost nearly sixty head to the sun and drought. I'm not about to let that happen again. George Timbledee is a hydrologist from Denver City, and Colonel Samuel Harrison is with the army engineers. Together, with the sweat of the extra men I've hired, they're raising a dam across the mouth of Thunder Canyon."

Stovill's face remained unmoved. "You said it was going to be hard work."

"Still doesn't bother you?"

"No, but it sounds as if you'd be better served hiring a gang of coolies instead of temperamental cowboys."

McSween leaned across the table and tapped an inch-long cylinder of gray ash from the tip of his cigar. "Already tried. Seems the railroad hires them up fast as they can unload them in San Francisco. You'll ride out with Chad in the morning. He'll set you straightways with Harrison."

"This place, this Thunder Canyon. You're planning on filling it with water?"

"I thought I made that plain enough?"

"Well, yes, you did. I was just curious. How large a reservoir you going to make of it?"

"As large as I can."

"The whole canyon?"

Chad said, "Thunder Canyon runs back about thirty miles. According to Timbledee about all we can fill with the dam we're building is maybe three miles. More than enough for our needs."

"So, very little really," Stovill said.

"I reckon, when you judge it by its full length." Chad shrugged. "Nothing back there to be concerned about."

McSween said, "Any other questions, Stovill?"

A sudden smile replaced his thoughtful

scowl. "Just one thing, sir."

"And that is?"

"I'd be happy if you'd call me Alex."

McSween tapped off another round of ash. "Very well, Alex it is." He stood, went to a tall oak cabinet and returned carrying a crystal decanter and three glasses. "As the old saying goes, business before pleasure. I judge our business is taken care of. Care to join me in a little pleasure?"

Chat took a glass and sipped, letting the whiskey fill his mouth with a warm, peaty flavor. It was Scotch, McSween's favorite, brought over from Scotland at considerable expense. After a while the mood turned easy and relaxed and the conversation drifted back to Harvard and Yale and places back east Chad had never heard about. He listened to them carry on, watching Stovill in the light from the chandelier overhead, aware of a certain uneasiness he wasn't able to put a finger on.

He dismissed the feeling and at the same time dismissed himself. Deep down inside him he knew what was bothering him. At least, he thought he knew.

CHAPTER 5

Stars flung across the cloudless heavens flickered like a thousand tiny campfires when Chad stepped out onto the porch looking for Libby. She wasn't there, but Eric was, sitting on the top step, his head craned back to the night sky.

An October breeze washed across the plains; a friendly wind coming from the east and the warm flats, not the cool mountains to the west. Pleasantly warm for so late in the season. But this was Colorado and that could all change in a moment.

Eric looked up from the porch step. "Hi, Chad."

He sat beside the boy. "What're you doing, pard?"

"Looking at the stars. Sure are a whole lot of them."

Chad followed the boy's gaze. "Sure are. Reckon more than a fellow can count." He listened to crickets chirping under the porch, caught the dark flicker of a bat out of the corner of his eye.

"That's not so, Chad. My teacher told us a man who lives in Germany counted more than three hundred thousand of them and wrote their names all down in a book called a catalog, only, it ain't a real catalog like what you'd order long handles or butter churns or a rifle out of. But he called it a catalog anyway. He didn't give them real names, either, just a bunch of numbers, but he called them names."

"You wouldn't be greening this old cowhand, would you, pard?"

Eric's eyes went wide. "Gosh, no, Chad. It's what he told us. I don't reckon I even know how big a number three hundred thousand is."

"Big enough to choke on. If I had to guess, I'd say it was the number three with a whole trainload of aughts behind it."

"Five, to be precise," Libby answered from behind them. She sat next to Eric. "A three followed by five zeros. What are you two talking about?"

"We was talking about the stars, Ma."

"Were."

"What?"

"You *were* talking about the stars. *Was* is singular and *we* is plural. The two have to

54

agree or you are using incorrect grammar."

"Gee whiz, Ma. I can't even relax at home."

"Eric G. Russman! You watch your language."

Chad grinned. "Eric was telling me there are over three hundred thousand stars up there, but I have a notion the hombre who counted them must have got sleepy eyes toward the end and counted a few more than once. The way I figure it, that many stars would make the night sky bright as high noon."

Eric shook his head. "Some of 'em you can't see without a thing called a telescope. Like a spyglass only bigger. There's even a machine that can track the stars they can't see — track them clear across the sky while the earth is a spinning." He thought a moment. "How you suppose they do that, Chad?"

Eric might as well have asked him how to fly. He gave the question some consideration all the while seeing a smirk on Libby's face. "I don't rightly know how they can do that, son, but I can tell you how to track an Arapaho in the dead of night on a week-old trail. First thing is, no matter how clever that Injun is, he's still gonna leave signs."

"Oh, Chad, there ain't no more wild

Indians to track. They've all been tamed, and anyway, Grandpa already told me all about Indian fighting. Say, I bet that Mr. Stovill would know!"

Chad winced. Eric hadn't meant harm by the remark, just the same his words stung. Ruefully, Chad admitted to himself that Stovill probably could answer Chad's questions. The man appeared ready to handle most situations. The thought rankled and he tried not to let the sudden bitterness he felt show. But Libby could always tell when a thing was bothering him.

"Eric, you have homework to do."

"Oh, Ma."

"It's time to get started. I'll be in later to see how you're doing."

"All right. See you later, Chad." He scuffed toward the door.

"And don't bother your grandpa or Mr. Stovill, hear?"

"I hear."

Eric went inside and Libby took Chad's arm and moved closer. "He didn't mean it, Chad."

"Mean what?" Pride was an almighty stumbling block for him. Always had been.

Libby squeezed his arm. "Don't try that on me, Mr. Larimer. I know you too well. Eric is just a boy, a boy learning there's a big wide world out there beyond the borders of his grandfather's ranch. The old things, the familiar things that have been his world all his life are no longer intriguing. He's seeing new horizons, learning there is more to life than the Rocking S."

Libby had a way of striking to the heart of a matter. Measuring his own worth through the eyes of a nine-year-old boy was about as useless as putting shoes on a three-legged horse. He ground the stump of the cigar beneath his boot. "I seem to recall the mention of a moonlight stroll."

"Chadwick Larimer. I declare you've more strut than a peacock. You can't admit your feelings were wounded."

"Let's walk." He took her hand and moved away from the house, the silence between them heavy, and made only more so by the chirping crickets and booming toads. They strolled toward a line of cottonwood trees along a stream that had its beginnings in the mountains and wound its way through miles of high country to finally tumble down into Thunder Canyon.

"When I was a boy I'd sit on my grandpa's knees listening to his stories about how he and my grandmother fought their way west. Back then all a boy needed to know about stars was how to read 'em like a compass so he didn't ride in a circle. It wasn't important to know how many of them there were in the sky. What was important was to have the sense to stay off ridgetops when in Indian country and those stars brightened the sky." He went quiet, recalling how it had been when he was a boy. "Maybe I tried counting 'em, I don't remember, but knowing how many wasn't important. Knowing how to use them was what mattered. Today kids don't care about the past, about common sense. They make life complicated."

"I think you're making life complicated, Chad."

He grunted. "Trouble with book learning is it clouds your vision. A person whose brain is filled with useless facts don't see simple truth in life. Good and bad become all mixed up until no one can tell the difference between 'em."

Libby didn't answer him at once. "You're a philosopher too, like Father. Don't scowl at me like that. Maybe you're right about good and bad getting all mixed up. Is that really bad? Life isn't all one way or the other. Never has been, even when you were a boy. There is a storybook character who could only see it one way or the other. His name was Don Quixote, and in his own way, he was a philosopher too. In some ways, you two are alike."

"Don who?"

She laughed. "Quixote. But he was only a made-up person in a book written a very long time ago by a man named Cervantes." Libby stopped and then stood on her toes and kissed him quite unexpectedly. "It isn't important, Chad."

Chad took her into his arms and their lips came together. She was both soft and firm beneath his hands and she did not resist him.

CHAPTER 6

Seldom would the sun catch Chad rising like it did the next morning. Usually it was the other way round. Sleeping past six o'clock felt like the best part of the day had been wasted. He swung his legs out of bed, stretched, then dressed hurriedly and stepped out onto the tiny front porch of the little house that was his alone to live in.

The sky was brightening, high clouds showing pink underbellies, the mountains to the west already catching the sun's light. He inhaled the crisp morning air — dry sage and grass, the nearby corral and barns . . . and coffee.

Chad stepped down from the porch and set his feet toward the bunkhouse. Inside, Cookie was at the sink washing dishes. McGrath and Peterson were still at the long table sipping the last of their coffee.

"Morning, Chad," Peterson said and McGrath waved.

Chad took a tin cup from the drying rack and filled it from a pot on the stove.

"Saved you some breakfast, Chad."

"Thanks, Cookie." Cookie wasn't his real name. It was Theodore Willoughby. But once he hired on to do kitchen chores, no one ever called him by that anymore.

Cookie lifted the heavy lid from a Dutch oven and fetched him out a pair of crisp biscuits, covered them with gravy then piled on a rack of bacon on the side. "You're a might late this morning?" He grinned. "Had a hard night?"

Although no one spoke openly about it, he and Libby were no secret around the bunkhouse. The men had eyes in their heads and they didn't miss much.

"Had paperwork to tend to," he said and let it go.

Cookie grinned wider. "Yep, I know all about that paperwork. Ever' month I gotta make out a supply list and head for town."

Chad had not seen Stovill when he came in and looked around the long room now. "Where's my new hand?"

The men at the table snickered and McGrath jerked a finger over his shoulder. "Sleepyhead is still sawing wood."

The clock showed six thirty. Chad set his cup and plate on the table and went through

61

the door to the sleeping quarters. Thirty bunks, fifteen on each side of the room lined the walls. All but one was empty. Stovill snored peacefully as if it was still the middle of night.

Chad gave him a shake. He snorted and rolled to his back coming slowly awake. Stovill stared at the ceiling a moment before becoming aware of Chad standing over him.

"Morning, Chad."

"Work days on the Rocking S generally begin at six, if not sooner."

"Six?" He levered himself onto his elbows and looked about the empty room, his view coming around to a nearby window where the morning light fell upon one of the empty beds. "What time is it?"

"Six thirty, and then some."

He offered a lame grin. "Guess I overslept."

"Guess so. Cookie has breakfast waiting." Chad wasn't of a mind to be too hard on the man seeing as he'd overslept a mite that morning himself. He returned to his breakfast and a few minutes later Stovill appeared at the doorway, dressed, wearing a six-gun and carrying his long-barreled rifle.

"See ya later, Chad." McGrath and Peterson dropped their dishes off on the sideboard on their way out.

Chad motioned Stovill to the table. "You won't be needing the hardware where you're going."

"I'd feel undressed without them. I'll bring them along if you don't mind, Chad."

The more Chad thought about it, the more he was certain Stovill was a greenhorn. "Bring 'em if you want, but you better grab some grub now seeing as you'll be living out at the building site for the next couple weeks and although Corky Rye is right clever with a Dutch oven, food out the back of a chuck wagon ain't near as satisfying as the grub Cookie serves up here in his fancy kitchen."

Chad heard Cookie scoff behind him. "I'm a amateur aside Corky. Corky flips the tastiest griddle cakes in all the Territory — err, I mean to say state now that Colorado am one."

Cookie would never admit it publicly, but here on the Rocking S he ran ramrod on the best cooking setup this side of a Harvey House. All he lacked were the fine-looking waitresses that Mr. Frederick Henry Harvey employed. On the other hand, Cookie wouldn't have tolerated their lovely presence behind his gleaming nickel-plated Baldwin stove anyway.

Stovill said, "I'll look forward to that."

Chad said to Stovill, "I suspect you'll be rolling out of your bedroll at dawn from here on. Harrison runs the site like a military encampment. He makes the men snap to, like they was soldiering."

"Can't wait," Stovill said dryly.

Chad smiled. He'd grown used to giving orders — to all but C. L. himself. The thought of working under Harrison's iron command was about as appealing as the notion of hauling dirt and piling it up across that canyon. If it was work that couldn't be done on the back of a good cow horse, Chad had little interest in it.

Cookie brought over a plate and cup, and Chad watched Stovill dig into the food with a healthy appetite and the look of a man who was liking what he was eating.

"Where'd you work before coming here?" Chad asked casually.

Stovill's view came up, glancing off of Chad, then returned to the biscuits and gravy. "Well, let's see." He sipped some coffee. "I spent three years at the Triple V up in Dakota Territory. Moved down to Texas afterwards and rode for Charlie Goodnight a while. Last place I worked was the Teaspoon."

Chad knew of the Teaspoon Ranch. "Bennet Overholster's place?"

"That's right," Stovill said and Chad detected a note of worry in his voice.

"I know the foreman, Sam Clay. Good man. You never slept past six on his watch."

Stovill laughed and the tension in his voice eased up. "No sir, Clay's a mule driver for sure."

Chad's shoulders tightened a mite. "Yep, he is." And he let the subject go. "After you finish up here you can go on down to the remuda and cut out a string of your own."

"I got a good horse, Chad."

Chad took a sip of his coffee. A man had the right to hide his past, even to lie a bit to keep it safe, but he never knew a wrangler to turn down a string of horses in favor of his own animal for range work — those few wranglers who could afford to own their own mount, that is. Sensible men rode what the outfit supplied, foregoing the expense of keeping and feeding an animal of his own.

"If you change your mind, you're entitled to a working string of seven. Maybe you might want to rope 'em out anyway, in case you decide later you want 'em."

"Sure. Soon as I get back."

"Your choice. Finish up and let's get moving. Thunder Canyon is a goodly ride from here."

Afterwards, he sent Stovill around for their

horses, then poured himself another cup of coffee and stood at the window watching him head for the corrals.

Cookie collected the dirty dishes and dumped them into the tub of soapy water. "He's a strange critter."

"It takes all kinds, Cookie."

He finished the last of his coffee and was leaving when Cookie said, "Chad, ain't old Matt Trevor foreman over at the Teaspoon?"

"Yep, he sure is." Chad left Cookie there wearing a puzzled look.

They rode away from the ranch house, turned onto a well-pounded trail that dipped into a narrow canyon and the ranch buildings disappeared behind them. Stovill was not in a talkative mood as their horses picked their way down a stony path then plodded past fat boles beneath the naked branches of cottonwood trees along the bottoms. Chad had his own thoughts to deal with. A while later the trail bent upward and their animals scrambled back to the flat plains, the brilliant green of the mountains farther off now.

Stovill broke the silence. "How far to Thunder Canyon?"

"Another hour." Chad's eyes scanned the far horizon. In another day — an earlier day

— he'd have been watching for signs. But, as Eric had pointed out the evening before, all the Indians in this place had been tamed. Even so, a part of him refused to give in to change.

"We still on Rocking S land?"

"Yep." The fact was, C. L. McSween's holdings were so large, Chad would have been in a hard place if forced to say this far was far enough and over there belonged to someone else.

"Are you sweet on Miss Libby?"

Chad reined to a stop and turned in his saddle. Stovill halted beside him, no hint on his face as to why he'd asked that. "You're getting a mite personal considering the short time you've been on the job."

Stovill raised his hand in peace. "No offense meant, Chad, but it's pretty plain by the way Miss Libby looks at you how she feels."

Chad eased back around and got his horse moving again, now at a lazy pace with Stovill alongside him. "I've known Libby Russman maybe fourteen . . . fifteen years. She's a fine woman and I ain't got nothing but respect for her. But if the truth be known, she had my eye long before she married."

"Miss Libby's easy on the eyes."

"You won't get an argument out of me."

"How'd her husband die?"

He looked across at Stovill and pondered just how much to say about the matter. But none of it was a secret and he'd hear the story soon enough. He might as well hear it straight rather than with the embellishments the tale had taken over the years. "The truth or the yarn Libby tells to keep it from Eric?"

"Truth."

Chad frowned, recalling that evening and the unanswered questions that still remained — and would remain — unless he confronted C. L. McSween, something he'd decided long ago he'd never do.

"Gary Russman was his name. In most respects a likable fellow if you overlooked the fact he was all the time grooming himself like a horse on parade. But that was a small thing. He was a lawyer from Denver City and came to Cañon City and hung his shingle out front of the new Santa Fe depot. Libby was fresh back from the East with her head filled with highfalutin ideas and an eye for respectability. Russman filled the bill and they were pretty soon hitched. Like I said, Russman was a likable gent. He had only one problem other than a wide streak of vanity." Chad glanced over at Stovill. "He bored quickly of sleeping in one bed. He liked to dip his line in strange waters."

Stovill frowned but Chad saw the grin fighting to break free. "I take it her husband's indiscretions did not sit well with Miss Libby?"

"What would you expect? Libby tried at first to ignore it but the word got around and she retreated. A prisoner in her own home. She knew people were talking, laughing like you wanted to do when you heard."

"Sorry."

"No need. It's how people react. I'm ashamed to say it, but I felt that way too. Maybe it was spite at having been rejected in favor of Russman."

"I take it then he did not die of natural causes?"

"It was bound to happen. McSween hated what Gary was doing to Libby. About two years ago Russman and a lady friend were warming the bedsheets when the lady's husband returned home unexpectedly. He'd been out of town on a trip and why he came home early, at just that moment, and carrying a revolver and . . . well, it's still a mystery.

"Whal, Russman took one look at the Navy Colt and sprang for an open window, naked as a newborn and proud as a stallion in a herd of mares. Out that window he flew with nothing but mother nature's own. And that hid very little from the eyes of the town that came awake at the noise of the ruckus. A military man might say he was in an exposed position. Russman headed for the nearest door he spied, which, to his misfortune, happened to belong to the privy out back of the house."

Chad shook his head, a little grin sneaking across his lips too. "He'd picked a poor place to hide. That husband was red-eye angry and out for revenge. He spied Russman going into that outhouse and slamming the door shut. Unfortunate hideout. I'll bet Russman was right surprised when he discovered where that doorway to safety led him — but then maybe he didn't have time to think about it. That jealous husband no sooner stopped in front of that closed door than he began emptying his revolver into it.

"When they got it open, Russman was sitting there on the stool with five bullet holes in him."

Stovill was grinning openly now. "I see why Miss Libby tells the yarn for Eric's sake. What came of the man who shot him?"

"Nothing. The judge said he had the right."

"I'd have done the same thing," Stovill said.

Chad turned his view back to the horizon. "He had the right, but the affair pulled Libby through the muck. That's all behind her now."

"And no one knows why the man came home unexpectedly?"

"No. And no one is asking."

They continued on. The even plod and sway of his horse lolled Chad, the warm October sun soothing upon his shoulders. His thoughts drifted onto other things as his eyes took in the beauty of the land. Here was something he understood. Here things worked together in predictable ways. No amount of book learning could teach a man more about the high plains than Chad already knew.

Giving free rein to his thoughts, like a good horse, they eventually returned to home — to Libby. He recalled something she'd said to him last night. His curiosity piqued he turned to Stovill. "You ever read any books?" At once he realized the foolishness of the question. Of course the man had read books! Had Stovill been a regular wrangler . . . Something in that line of thinking nagged at him.

"I've read a few," he said, taking the question in easy stride.

Chad swallowed down his foolishness and

said, "Ever read 'bout a fellow named Don Coyote?" He turned his face away so that Stovill wouldn't see his embarrassment.

"Don Quixote? Yes, I've read it. Why do you ask?"

Well, he'd brought it up and he was going to see it through in spite of how he now felt foolish. "Last night Libby said I was sort of like this Coyote fellow. When I asked about him she only laughed as if it were nothing."

"Oh, is that all." He smiled. "I wouldn't worry about it, Chad. Don Quixote was a fictional character who had some very definite ideas of right and wrong, of honor and duty. These notions were so strong in him, he couldn't see past them to the real world around him. Nobody can ever be Don Quixote, but I suspect if you search deep enough, you're likely to find a little of Don Quixote in most every man. And that's not such a bad thing, now is it?"

"No, reckon not." Chad still didn't fully understand as he turned back in his saddle and looked ahead. "Someday I might have to read me that book."

The grand earthen structure curved in a great arch from one steep and jagged wall to the other. A full one hundred and eighty feet long, the dam now rose to a height of almost twenty-five feet, and this was only the first of three planned levels.

Beneath this mound, Colonel Harrison had built a huge culvert. An iron rod topped with an iron wheel very much like a brakeman's wheel, rose from the culvert like a spindly rusty flower. At the moment, water tumbled freely through the culvert but within a month that brakeman's wheel would be spun down, choking the torrent to a trickle, and McSween's dam would begin to fill.

From where Chad sat astride his horse at the canyon's rim, the workers below looked like so many ants building a hill.

Stovill didn't say anything at first, his eyes wide at the sight. Then he blew out an appreciative whistle. "Mr. McSween wasn't kidding when he said he was building a dam."

"It's important to him. Someday he'll have the biggest spread in the state and this dam will be the reason why. Water is worth more than gold in this country." They followed the trail along the rimrock and then down a steep road to the construction camp at the dam's base. Seen from this angle, the dam appeared taller than it had from above. Stovill craned his neck toward the roadway along the top where oxcarts filled with dirt moved in and out in a steady procession.

Chad rode to the chuck wagon where some of the men were eating lunch. He introduced Stovill to them then moved off a small distance to where a lone man sat in the shade upon a three-legged stool, balancing a plate on his knees, a cup of coffee in one hand.

Timbledee looked up with a start, then smiled broadly. "Chad. You startled me." He was a short man with round steel-rimmed eyeglasses, a narrow mouth and broad head. The black hair that remained was in a rapid retreat. "What brings you out?" He pushed the spectacles up the bridge of his nose then rebalanced the plate, which had almost upended itself at his start.

"Brought you another back to bust." Chad grinned. "This here is Mr. Alexander Stovill the Second, but never mind the fancy handle. He gets uppity if you don't call him Alex." He turned to Stovill. "This is Mr. George Timbledee. He's from Denver City here to keep an eye on things and make sure we don't do anything with the water that the state of Colorado don't like."

Timbledee laughed. "You're making the state out to be an ogre peeking into people's backyard. Pleased to meet you Mr. Stovill — err, I mean Alex. Soon as the colonel gets back we'll find a place for you."

"Where's Harrison?" Chad asked, looking around.

Timbledee waved toward the dam. "Somewhere on the other side, inspecting one thing or another. He runs a spit-shine campaign here. One might wonder if he isn't expecting President Hayes to show up for an inspection." He laughed.

"It's his upbringing," Chad said. "He can't help himself."

"I reckon the army will do that to a man," Timbledee noted with an air of pity in his voice.

"We'll get some grub and wait for him."

"See you later." Timbledee went back to his lunch. Chad and Stovill dismounted and took their horses to a picket line. They fetched themselves some food from the chuck wagon and found shade against the canyon's wall under which to eat. A little while later Colonel Harrison appeared at the top of the dam and started down the steep slope, digging in his heels to keep a footing.

Chad brought Stovill over. The Colonel seemed pleased with his new recruit, issued him a regulation shovel and gave him his marching orders. Stovill tromped after the

colonel, casting a bemused look over his
shoulder at Chad as he left.

CHAPTER 7

Chad rode up the stream leaving the busy construction site behind him. Alone now and grateful for the solitude, Chad heard the rippling water sing a soothing song accompanied by a rustling breeze and an occasional chattering bird. As he worked his way up into Thunder Canyon looking for strays, his eye occasionally pulled skyward to watch a hawk making long spirals on the warm air rising from the flatlands beyond the canyon's rim. Up there the ground was sun-warmed, but down here great slabs of shade reached across the canyon's floor. The breeze that found its way along the stream was chilled, scented with cedar and juniper.

A coiled rattlesnake on a sandstone ledge warmed itself in a slash of sunlight that managed to find a way through the shade. The snake lifted its flat head and licked out a tongue as Chad rode past. Its tail flicked once or twice sending out a hollow rattle like a seed gourd, then it lowered its head again. Chad was no threat.

An hour passed, and then two, and not a single cow. He was beginning to suspect none of McSween's beeves had wandered back into the canyon. Off to his left a dark slit marked the entrance to another small side canyon. From it, a trickle of water cut a mossy green rivulet down to the larger stream. Probably nothing back up there. All the others he'd investigated had been empty. But he had to make a quick inspection to be sure and he turned his horse toward it putting the sun on his back.

Eyes bent to the ground, Chad reined in sharply and stared at a well-worn trace. It wasn't cows. Horses. One was shod the other wasn't. He sat very still, studying the tracks that led straight into the side canyon. His horse snorted, scenting something. Another horse? Chad's ears sharpened; the trickle from the canyon, the stream behind him, wind in the branches of a cottonwood tree . . . and now something else.

Tink . . . tink . . . tink.

Not the sound an animal would make. Metal striking rock? Prospectors? No valuable minerals he knew of in this part of Colorado. He slipped his Sharps rifle from the scabbard and swung noiselessly out of the saddle. The sound grew louder as the deep shade closed in about him. It was definite now, and coming from up ahead where the canyon narrowed. He paused and lowered the breech of his rifle to check that it was loaded. It was, and he continued up the narrow cut, keeping near the steep wall, silent as a spirit, eyes and nose alert.

As far as he knew, there'd never been any mining in the area. A little coal in Cañon City maybe, but that was all. There were plenty of flint outcroppings, and it was common to find old arrowheads washed down from the slopes. Sometimes he'd spy signs that Indians had passed through, but they didn't work flint anymore. Iron arrowheads were easy enough to come by nowadays, if they'd even bother with such things now that caplock rifles surplused after the war were so plentiful and cheap.

The faint odor of a cook fire threaded its way from the canyon depths — cedar.

Tink . . . tink . . . tink, tink.

Chad halted beyond an outcrop of sandstone and listened. He'd heard similar sounds once while watching Indian boys chipping flint in the old ways; the elders trying to keep the past from being forgotten. But he didn't think it was that. This was different somehow.

He inched forward.

"Dammit!" a man's voice cried sharply.

Chad stepped around the outcropping. A lone man with his back to Chad was on his knees, hunched over something. The man held a queer-looking hammer with a long spike on one end, at the moment poised in midair. As Chad watched, the hammer struck three quick, carefully aimed blows at a bit of rock.

A short ways off stood a horse and donkey, tethered to a stunted piñon tree on a stony slope of rock. He eyed the animals then a level patch of ground not far off where water from a spring pooled. A frown shaped his lips, and he glanced back at the man now busily sweeping the ground with a brush that looked like something Cookie used to clean the ashes from his stove.

On the other side of the cook fire was a bedroll and a couple open packs. Against a rock leaned a rifle. Chad had never seen anything quite like this. More than a little curious, he settled the rifle into the crook of his arm, watched a moment longer, then said, "What in blazes are you up to, mister?"

The man spun about, startled, nearly losing his balance. He caught himself, his eyes big and fixed upon the rifle in Chad's arms. Those round eyes moved to Chad's face and he swallowed hard. "I didn't hear you."

"That's plain enough. Who are you?"

"Me?"

"I don't see nobody else about. What's your name?"

"Cobsworth." He stood. Cobsworth was a tall, slender man with long arms. His Adam's apple vigorously worked the top button of his smudged white shirt. "Samuel Cobsworth. Who might you be?"

"You alone up here?" Chad glance around again.

"Ye—" Cobsworth stopped and Chad could see him thinking about it. "I mean, no. Err, my partner ought to be back almost any instant now."

Chad glanced at the single bedroll and grinned. "You and your partner sleeping together?"

"No! Err, he . . . he took his stuff with him."

Chad shook his head. "Mr. Cobsworth, you are lying to me. You are alone up here. Now, tell me what you're doing."

"Nothing . . . nothing at all . . ."

"You're still lying. Whatcha you working at there?" He climbed the slope and peered down where Cobsworth had been picking and sweeping. There wasn't anything there but some old cow bones. "You're digging bones?"

"Well, if you must know, yes." He stood a little taller and hooked his thumbs through his galluses, puffing his chest a bit. "I'm a paleontologist."

The word ricocheted off Chad's brain without making a dent of understanding. He considered him narrowly. "What's that? Some sort of religion?"

"Certainly not," he retorted, tugging with indignation at his suspenders. "I am a scientist."

"Scientist?" Chad scratched the back of his neck. He'd heard of them, but never met one. Just the same, what fuzzy picture he'd ever formed of a scientist did not at all square with the man standing in front of him. Chad deliberated upon the worn trousers with dirty knees, upon the dingy shirt and worn elbows. Somehow he envisioned something a bit more impressive — a man with a pipe in his mouth, a pencil and leather notebook in hand, and maybe a glass pinched between the lids of one eye. "Then why are you out here digging up old cow bones?"

"Cow bones!" He nearly choked on the word, and his face was red as a brothel's porch. "Cow bones," he reiterated as if he could not believe what he had heard. "I'll have you know, sir, that I'm on the verge of a significant discovery. Perhaps the grandest yet in the field of paleontology."

There was that word again, and the way he said it, Chad wasn't certain it was not some sort of new religion.

"These . . . these *cow bones* as you disparagingly refer to them may very well be the remains of a diplodocus, although the more I uncover I am inclined to believe they may very well belong to an entirely new and yet unnamed species. Cow bones! Cow bones, indeed."

Cobsworth went on using words Chad didn't hardly understand, and Chad leaned back a bit in case the man might bust a vein or something. Cobsworth was a peculiar critter. He had a solid, sharply defined jaw, while the rest of him was more or less shaped up like a fence rail — except for broad shoulders that hinted at well-developed muscles beneath the shirt. Though willowy, Chad sensed a resiliency about the man. Just the same, for all the outward solidity, he was upsettable as a matron dancing atop a stool in a roomful of mice. His voice, which had begun a pleasant baritone, reached now for notes high enough to bust an ear. He looked to be about forty years old and had all the makings of a tolerable handsome gent, but his excitable rant wasn't doing him any favors.

Chad set the butt of his rifle on the ground and leaned on the barrel and waited for Cobsworth to settle down. The man took a long ragged breath and pulled a handkerchief from his pocket to mop his forehead.

"You gonna be all right, mister?"

"Yes . . . yes, I think so." Cobsworth shot him a peeved look. "Just who are you?"

"My name's Chadwick Larimer. I'm foreman of the Rocking S Ranch. This here hunk of real estate you're trespassing on belongs to C. L. McSween."

Cobsworth finished mopping his head and shoved the handkerchief into a pocket. "I'm sorry if I've wandered where I don't belong. I did not realize anyone owned this stretch of desert."

"Desert?" He'd seen the Sonoran and he'd heard of the death trails across the waterless stretches of the Mojave, both true deserts in their own right, but he'd never heard anyone refer to this land as desert. "This here is cattle country, Mr. Cobsworth. We have good grass and a fair amount of water — when we ain't having a drought."

Cobsworth shook his head. "Desert. Look at any vegetation map. This is the northern extension of the Upper Sonoran Desert."

Chad took a menacing step forward and Cobsworth scrambled back, half stumbling over a rock. "I don't care what fancy name you put to it, this here is prime cattle country, and it all belongs to the Rocking S Outfit. And you're still trespassing. Pack them animals and find someplace else to dig up cow bones."

"I can't leave."

"Yes, you can and yes, you will."

His finger trembled as it pointed at the cow bone. "But my discovery."

"What discovery? Them bones are all over the place. Listen, Mr. Cobsworth, a long time ago the Injuns what used to live here used to stampede whole herds of buffalo over these cliffs. That's how they hunted enough meat to feed their people. What you got there ain't nothing but old cow bones — whal, maybe buffalo bones. It's all the same. Why, over at Red Canyon a man might trip over these all day long."

"Really?" Cobsworth said, momentarily intrigued.

Chad flung an arm in disgust. A single-minded dandy was all Cobsworth was and he didn't want to waste any more time on him. "I give you an hour to pack up and leave before I throw you out of here." He turned, then remembered something. "And another thing. Next time you're digging up cow bones, tether your animals where the ground is level and there's water and grass for 'em. How would you like to be standing on your tiptoes in loose rubble all day long?"

Cobsworth glanced at the horse and mule. "I didn't realize . . ."

"A dandy like you probably wouldn't." He swung around and started out of the canyon.

"Please, just one minute more," Cobsworth called after him. "Please. I want to show you something, Mr. Larimer."

Chad took a breath and turned back. Cobsworth was pointing at a lumpy gray canvas tarpaulin. "All right. Then you're leaving."

Cobsworth flung back the canvas and as Chad half expected, there lay a pile of old bones. "So what? I've seen bones before. Now, get packing."

"You didn't *look* at them!"

Admittedly, he'd just glanced at them and seen what he'd expected to see. Now he looked again and something began grinding uncomfortably in his gut. They weren't like any cow bones he'd ever seen before. There was something very different about these. Cobsworth knelt beside one exceptionally long bone and ran a hand along it like it

86

was a rare jewel or a bar of glittering gold.

"This is a femur," he said, then perhaps seeing the blank look in Chad's eyes added, "a leg bone."

Chad's heart was hitting his chest harder than usual and he didn't know why. It was plainly a leg bone, at least it was shaped like one. But it was eight feet long and thick as a young tree. It didn't look soft or flaky like old bones looked. This had the appearance of hard, solid rock.

"I'll wager a month's salary you've never seen a cow bone like this one, Mr. Larimer."

Chad didn't reply. His eyes were showing him something that couldn't be. He'd ridden past lots of old cow bones, but never had he ever seen one bone bigger than a whole cow!

CHAPTER 8

Cobsworth covered the bones, arranging the canvas with care, tucking in the ends. He stood and studied Chad a moment. "What I've discovered here is quite important work. I and a handful of scientists are breaking new ground in the young field of paleontology — literally." He grinned as if he'd made a joke. If he had, Chad didn't catch the meaning. Cobsworth cleared his throat. "This discovery may prove more important than anything Professor Cope has found to date."

Chad's thoughts were still back on that bone, his eyes lingering upon the gray canvas mound. It wasn't only the size of the thing that had left him without any word to speak, it was what it had been made of. Stone. He'd put a hand on it and felt it for himself. Living bone changed into solid rock. What was it Cobsworth had called it? Fossilization? And what was it he'd said?

They were old, real old — millions old. Chad didn't know how many aughts that number was, but it was a sight bigger than Eric's star count.

"I have some coffee on the fire, Mr. Larimer."

Chad pulled his eyes from the canvas. "Okay."

"Good."

Chad put his thoughts back on the present. "But first I'll see to those animals."

Cobsworth hunkered down by the smoldering cook fire and stirred the coals, feeding them dry trigs. Chad moved the animals and staked them on a level area near water and grass. He returned and took a cup from Cobsworth.

"What did you say that critter is called?"

"I didn't say for certain. It resembles the diplodocus — shorter front legs than rear, long whip-like tail and so forth. The teeth I'm finding out as I uncover parts of the skull appear to be simple haplodont teeth."

Chad tasted the coffee, not following all of what Cobsworth was saying.

"But the proportions are not correct. This appears not to be a diplodocus but a much larger animal. Hence, I believe I've discovered a new species."

"How big?" Chad tried to shape up in his

mind an animal with an upper leg bone the length of the one he'd been shown.

"My guess is, perhaps as long as eighty feet."

Chad whistled. "That's longer than the bunkhouse. A man would be sore fixed to rope one of 'em for the iron."

Cobsworth grinned. "You'd have to ride a locomotive and use steel bridge cable for a rope. And I'd still put my money on old George over there." He jabbed a thumb at the pile.

"George?"

"I have to give them names. It makes it personal that way. When you're out alone for months at a time with nothing but long-dead creatures for company, it helps."

"You've been at this work a long time?" Though Cobsworth was a peculiar hombre, he was easy to get to know and not such a bad fellow — so long as he didn't get excited.

"About ten years, off and on. Most of the time I teach paleontology at Haverford College in Pennsylvania, but every so often I managed to land a grant from my old friend, Professor Edward Cope. When I do, I'm off again for a few months to see what I can find. The West is turning out to be a treasure house of dinosaur bones."

"How long you been here in Thunder Canyon?"

"Almost three months. Thunder Canyon? Is that the name of this place?"

"It's what Injuns called it a long time ago. They used different words for it, their own words."

"I had a student helping me the first month so I wasn't alone. He left to return to school — fall semester, you know. I sent back a report with him of what I found here. A field book of notes and some drawings and measurements. I expect Professor Cope to be coming here himself for a look."

Another college man? It seems of recent, the countryside was flush with 'em, and they all were showing up at the Rocking S. McSween didn't count even though he once taught law at Harvard in the '30s, seeing as he had beaten them all out here by more'n forty years, but there was Stovill who just turned up. A Yale college man passing himself off as a cowboy. He could ride all right, but Chad had a suspicion that was as far as Stovill's cowboying went. Now Samuel Cobsworth. A bone digger from Pennsylvania.

He shrugged off a worrisome feeling. It seems he'd grown a thin skin of late, and that wasn't his usual nature. Besides, when it came down to it, he could best 'em all in matters where it counted. With one hand tied behind his back. They were Eastern dandies, both of 'em. Book learning didn't amount to cowslip when it came to fending for one's self in hard country.

Chad considered Cobsworth. He seemed a likable gent whose only real fault was that he was so wrapped up in his work, and that was his right. "Who's this Cope fellow?"

Cobsworth blinked out of his coffee cup. "Edward Drinker Cope, of course. Surely you've read of him in the newspapers?"

"Reckon not," Chad said flatly.

"Well, Professor Cope is a paleontologist, like me, only he's famous. One of the foremost scientists in the country. Every couple months he publishes and describes a new fossil discovery. Certainly you've read of the feud between him and Professor Marsh?"

Chad looked hard at Cobsworth. "I can't read." There. It was out.

Cobworth's face pinkened some. "I'm sorry. I didn't mean anything by it, Mr. Larimer."

"I know."

"It was foolish for me to have assumed —"

"Forget it."

Flustered, he reached for the pot. "More coffee?"

Chad stuck out his cup and Cobsworth filled it, his hand some unsteady. "How long did it take you to learn reading, Mr. Cobsworth?"

"Learn?" He shrugged and replaced the pot. "I don't know. I began reading as a child."

A child. Chad frowned and sipped his coffee then stared at the brown liquid a moment. "I better be getting back to work." He stood.

"I can teach you."

Chad had started toward his horse. He turned back. "Thanks, but I ain't a child no more. There isn't enough time. You need to get packing, Mr. Cobsworth. Your hour is running."

Cobsworth leaped to his feet. "But I told you, I can't leave. My work! I thought you understood?"

"You've found yourself something of a curiosity here, I admit, but C. L. McSween is building a dam across the canyon and in a couple months all this will be lake bottom. Your bones, these trees, the animals that make this canyon home, it will all be gone. I'm sorry, but that's the way it is. McSween has three thousand head of beef needing water and this is his land."

Seeing Cobsworth's stunned face brought a pang of regret, but McSween had cattle to think about and all Cobsworth had were a pile of dried bones. It wasn't necessarily fair, but then life rarely was. Pausing at the outcrop that had first concealed him, Chad look back. Cobsworth hadn't moved, looking as devastated by this turn of events as the summer's drought had been to McSween. Chad felt the frown shape his lips. Cobsworth had to leave, no changing that, but maybe not today, not this hour? "We start filling this canyon in three weeks. You can stay until then."

"I need at least three months."

Chad shook his head. "There isn't the time."

He swung into his saddle and headed back to the main cut of Thunder Canyon, trying to bury Samuel Cobsworth somewhere out of mind. But he could not shake free of the sight of that huge leg bone from the past. As he moved down the stream back the way he'd come, he realized, oddly, that it wasn't cows he was thinking about. It was a mighty creature eighty feet from nose to tail that rumbled across the ancient plains of his imagination.

The high clouds had shaded to a dirty gray and the sky was a deep sapphire blue by the time Chad came around the last bend and saw the dark berm of the dam ahead. It was all in shadow now, empty oxcarts atop it. He urged his horse up a rubble trail and down the other side where campfires greeted him.

He rode past men lazing about after a hard day's labor, too exhausted to care who was passing by. Some managed a nod, others a brief wave. Most were too tired to notice him. He reined in by the chuck wagon and swung out of the saddle.

"Evening Chad," Corky Rye, the camp cook, said. "Want some vittles?"

"Those beans smell good, and the coffee." Chad turned the reins around a wheel rim while Corky ladled a pile of beans onto a tin plate.

"Spiced apples?"

"No thanks. This will do fine." Chad spied Stovill sitting among a group of men by one of the campfires. "How's the new man getting along?"

Corky chuckled and stroked the gray stubble on his chin. "He's got a winning way about him. Fitted himself right in like fingers in a glove."

"Yep." Chad forked up some beans. "He do have a way of finding a comfortable perch in short time." He set the hot coffee cup on the edge of his plate and strolled to the campfire.

"Chad," Stovill called out when he looked over and saw him approaching. "Come over and join us."

Chad found a seat on a log and set his cup on the ground between his boots.

"Find those cows?" Stovill asked.

"Nary a one. Nothing up there but rattle-snakes."

"That's all?"

One of the men laughed. "That's more'n 'nough for me."

Chad studied Stovill in the flickering firelight, finding in the man's face an uncommon eagerness, a seeking in his eyes. Maybe he was reading more into it than was really there. "Yep, that's all. What did you expect I might find up there?"

Stovill shrugged and smiled amiably. "With a name like Thunder Canyon, hopefully mystery and adventure."

Chad grinned. "No mystery and no adventure, I'm afraid."

Terry Filbert tossed a twig into the fire.

"Alex says we had us some rustlers over to Coal Creek."

"Ran into some men with a running iron. Got kinda rollicky for a while. Fortunate for me and Eric, Alex showed up with that long-barrel rifle."

Filbert shook his head. "He told us all about it. Like to have seen it. That was some crackerjack shooting."

"It was nothing much," Stovill said, sounding humble.

Chad said, "Maybe Alex will give you a demonstration? He totes that rifle along with him wherever he goes."

"Don't make more of it than there was. I'm only happy I was near enough to hear and be able to help."

Chad worked at his food sorting through his feelings. He couldn't put a finger on the reason why, but the feeling he was most aware of was resentment, even though Stovill had done nothing wrong. Maybe that was it? Everything he did was just right. To Chad's way of thinking, there was something unnatural about that.

"You staying on tonight, Chad?" Filbert asked.

"No. Soon as I'm finished eating I'm heading back to headquarters."

■ ■ ■ ■

Chad tossed the grounds from the bottom of his cup into the fire and sat a moment watching the embers grow red again where the coffee had darkened them. He stood. "I need to get moving."

"So long, Chad," Filbert said.

Stovill looked up. "Tell Mr. McSween and Miss Libby hello from me."

"Sure." Chad started off then paused and looked back. "Any of you fellows ever hear of a critter called a dinosawer?"

They each allowed they had not, all except Stovill who began scratching at the ground with a stick. "I think I heard of them, once. Must have been at school. Don't know anything about them." He jabbed the stick and it snapped, looking up through narrowed eyes. "Where'd you pick up that word, Chad?"

"I must have heard the word once, myself," Chad replied turning away and feeling Stovill's stare burning his back all the way to his horse.

CHAPTER 9

Since the both of them knew the way home there was no good reason why the both of them should work at getting them there. That being the situation, Chad gave it over to his horse and let his thoughts drift. The air was cool beneath the stars, but not unpleasant. When a coyote gave out a lonely yelp in the distance, Chad wondered how Cobsworth was faring now, alone in the blackness of the canyon with only the bones of a monster dead and buried for more centuries than a man could hardly count for company. His thoughts wandered and eventually came around to what Cobsworth had said about reading. He'd begun as a child, probably even younger than when Eric had begun to learn how. A frown tugged the corners of his lips when he thought of his own childhood.

His mother never knew reading and writing and neither did Grandpa William and

Grandma Sarah. In the one-room cabin where the four of them lived, reading and writing had no place. Milking cows, planting crops and tending traplines did.

Had his father been able to read? He never knew the trapper who happened upon their cabin one cold winter's night in the middle of the most fierce blizzard of the year. Chad's grandparents took the man in and he stayed until the spring brought new life to the valley. He left when the snows had melted and swelled the river, but a part of him remained, growing inside Chad's mother.

The trapper never returned, and although Chad grew to boyhood knowing nothing but love within the four walls of their cabin, there lingered a stigma he could never be shed of, and a certain man he was determined to someday find. It was that, mostly, and maybe a wanderlust bequeathed to him by an unknown father, that first called him to the mountains. He remembered his mother's tears as she waved good-bye to him. At age fourteen, he was ready strike out on his own with a Leman's caplock rifle over his arm and a scrawny mule packed with the few traps and gear his grandfather could afford to let him take.

But the beaver trade had already seen its

glory days, and Chad would have likely died right along with it if not for a fortunate friendship with a big mountain man with even bigger ideas about ranching. When McSween made the slide from trapper to rancher, he took Chad along with him. He cut the Rocking S out of an empty land, and after he'd built a house and bought a starter herd, he sent for his wife and daughter, who still lived in the East. He made Chad his foreman and it was well known he intended to leave a part of it to Chad someday.

But when Libby married Gary Russman, McSween felt duty-bound to make Russman his heir — for Libby's sake. He never liked Russman and the night his son-in-law died, McSween broke out the whiskey and passed it around like a man reprieved from the hangman's noose. Chad thought about that night a lot, and about the woman's husband returning of a sudden, carrying a revolver. Chad never brought it up, though. And for his part, McSween never did either, although McSween knew more than he ever let on.

The moon crawled higher into the sky, spreading a ghostly veil across the land. He looked to the stars. Count them? How would he ever go about doing such a thing?

Eric's question still befuddled him, but he knew where he might find the answer. Books. Books could tell him all he needed to know. A bitter spirit filled him. He was too old to learn now.

But Cobsworth had offered to teach him?

Would he have done so if it was beyond him?

Bile rose and burned his throat. No. There wasn't time enough, and he wasn't a bright-eyed boy anymore. A day late and a dollar short. A fitting epitaph for a tombstone.

The moon was high overhead when he spied the lights from the Rocking S. By his starry clock he knew it was still early — nine thirty at the most — and by the bright lamplight pouring from the windows, Mc-Sween and Libby were still up and about. He rode under the Rocking S shingle and up to the house, turning the reins about the hitching rail and climbing the steps.

The door swung open in response to his knock and Libby stood there, framed in the doorway, looking lovely in the soft parlor light.

"Chad?" Her eyes sparkled. "We didn't expect you back tonight." She smiled and batted her eyelashes alluringly. Whether it was in playfulness or simply surprise, he didn't know, but it was flattering. "Don't tell me you rode all the way back tonight just to see me?"

He grinned at her. "All right, I won't."

She laughed and stepped aside for him to enter. "Father's in back cleaning that old rifle again. Why does he carry on over that old thing like he does? It's older than I am."

"Sentimental reason."

"Hum. You're probably right, Chad. A woman always comes in third place, right behind guns and horses."

It was Chad's turn to laugh. "I'm not too sure I would agree with that, Libby."

"Of course you wouldn't. You're a sweetheart. I'll get Father. Why don't you wait for him in his office?"

As Libby sashayed from the room, Chad knew for a fact guns and horses would never stand a chance against a woman like her.

He opened the door to McSween's office and there they were, waiting for him, leather bound and frowning, silent in their incriminations. He stared back at them and a thought entered his head. *It didn't have to be this way.* He swallowed hard and pushed himself across the room to face them like a man. Why did he always put flesh and bone on them? Why were they his adversary? The Injun in the woods. The gunman in the alley. Taking a breath, he removed one from the shelf, something he'd never thought to do in the past. It was thick and heavy, and although he could not read the name of it, he was pleasantly amazed at the floral design decorating the inside of it. There was a date, 1874. But that was all the book would allow him to know.

"Someday . . ."

"You taking up reading, Chad?" McSween's voice brought Chad's head around. The big man filled the doorway leaving only a hint of the blue-and-white wallpaper on the hallway wall behind him. In his hand was the dark Hawken rifle. Chad's memory flashed back to the first time he put eyes on the rifle and the great, bearded man who carried it.

McSween had been much younger then, still impressive in size, but it was the ice-blue eyes, sharp as an Arkansas toothpick, that Chad had noted first. It had been in a high mountain glade fresh with spring color, reds and yellows and white, and the knee-high columbine pale lavender in the morning sunlight. McSween strode across the field, hardly slowing to snatch Chad's rife from the tall grass. He eyed it critically then stood over Chad. He snorted, blowing out the corner of his mouth in a manner Chad would soon become accustomed to.

"It's no wonder, boy." His voice was a rumbling avalanche. "A peashooter rifle like this one will get you killed quicker than a scalp-hungry Injun." McSween bent over the grizzly bear that had fallen not two rods from Chad. "Whal, she's sure enough dead now. Looky there what you done. Why, that little bullet of yours only riled her up. Fortunate I seen it happen from over there." He pointed. Then he shook his rifle at Chad. "You need to get yourself a big fifty like this one, if you intend to wander in these here hills."

Being a lad of fifteen, Chad eyed the arrival of this newcomer with near the same terror he had known when that old grizzly bear had begun her charge. McSween towered over him a moment then laughed like thunder and offered Chad a hand up from the ground, and they'd been friends ever since.

Chad looked at the book and for an instant he felt just holding it was a transgression of sorts, like a drunk caught fetching out a hidden bottle. "I was . . . curious."

McSween took it from him and peered at the back of it. "*Littell's Living Age.* It's a weekly publication. This is the bound volume of those issues for the second half of eighteen seventy-four. Mostly contemporary

stories and articles. Some interesting reading."

"I'm sure it is."

"Here. Take it with you. I suspect you
know some of the words, and with effort,
you can learn the rest of them."

"I don't know . . ."

"Go ahead take it."

Chad hesitated then took the book from
McSween's hand. "Whal, maybe I can give
it a try."

"Libby can help you with it too." He gave
Chad a wink and leaned the rifle in the
corner behind his desk. Dropping into the
chair, he produced two cigars from the
humidor and motioned Chad to a chair.

"Didn't expect you'd be riding back
tonight." He bit off the end of his cigar and
struck a match. Chad moved his cigar into
the flame then leaned back while McSween
played the fire across his own.

"I ran across something I thought you
should know."

"What's that?"

"There's a man camped out up the canyon."

McSween looked puzzled. "What the devil
is he up to?"

"Digging up old bones."

"That's a mighty peculiar occupation,

Chad." He blew a cloud of smoke at the ceiling.

"I thought so too. He calls himself a paleo . . . paleo-on-something."

"Paleontologist?"

"That's the word."

"Humph! Grave robbers. They make an enterprise out of digging up the dead. You told him to make tracks, didn't you?"

"I did. He got all red in the face and pronounced that he'd found a special kind of critter called a dinosawer."

"A what?" McSween's eyes narrowed.

"He called it a dinosawer, and another name — a dippi-o-doccus, I think he said it was. It's some kind of king-size critter bigger than a bunkhouse. He claims a bunch of 'em used to herd up in these parts a long time ago."

"I don't care what he claims. He's got to go. If he don't, some grave robber will be digging *his* bones."

"I said he could stay till we start filling Thunder Canyon."

McSween gave a disgusted grunt. "You're more generous than I'd have been, Chad." His scowl deepened. "I don't suppose it will do any harm — so long as that bone digger is out of there when we start filling."

Chad wished now that he'd booted Cobsworth out as he had intended. "He'll be gone."

McSween shook his head, his voice losing its rancor. "Something about a man making a living that way — the dead should be allowed to rest in peace be they human or otherwise." He looked up sharply. "It isn't wise to disturb the dead."

Chad grinned. "Sounds like Injun talk to me, C. L. You spent too much time listening to them old tepee stories."

McSween pushed out his lower lip in a petulant pout. "Perhaps. But I believe some of it is true." A silence settled between them and Chad thought of Cobsworth busily removing a long dead thing from its rocky tomb. What would a Comanche think of such a thing? McSween's words changing subjects intruded on his thoughts. "How many beeves you find, Chad?"

"None. But I didn't get all the way back. Spent some time talking to Cobsworth. I'll head back to Thunder Canyon in the morning."

"Cobsworth? Is that the bone digger's name?"

"Samuel Cobsworth. Works with another bone digger by the name of Cope." He stood and glanced at the book in his hand, feeling odd taking it with him. "Better get some sleep if'n I'm going to get an early start. Good night."

Libby was rocking in the porch swing when he stepped out the front door. She beckoned him to sit beside her. "Now tell me what was so important to tell Father that you rode all the way back here tonight?"

The swing creaked under his weight, the air faintly scented with lilac, something that he hadn't noticed when she'd met him at the door earlier. "Ranch business. You wouldn't be interested."

"The ranch interests me, you know that. Why the secrecy?"

He'd not considered Cobsworth a secret, was surprised she saw it that way. When he finished telling her what he'd told Mc-Sween, Libby's eyes were blue flint. He half expected her to be more curious. Instead she was angry. "That man will have to leave the canyon. We can't delay filling the reservoir over some silly bones."

Her reaction surprised him. "I gave Cobsworth three weeks. He'll be gone. What's wrong, Libby?"

"Wrong? I'd have thought you would understand how important this dam is to Father and me . . . and the ranch." Her eyes fell upon the book in his hands. "What's that?"

"It's a book." He knew before the words left his mouth that wasn't what she was asking. Too late to take 'em back now.

"I know it's a book, silly. Why do you have it?"

He stiffened a little at the accusation he detected in her tone of voice. "I figured maybe I could learn to read it."

"Read? You've never talked about it before."

"Whal, I just got to thinking it might come in handy someday." Why did he feel he had to explain his motives? And why did it make him feel somehow guilty of a crime doing so?

Libby laughed. "That's silly. You know enough to do your job here quite well enough without bothering with that. If there is any reading that needs to be done, Father does it, or I do. Anyway, you're too old to . . . Chad, where are you going?"

He'd stood and started down the steps. He didn't look back, tried not to let the hurt sound in his words. "It's been a long day, Libby, and I got another one ahead of me tomorrow." He untied his horse and started toward the barn.

Libby hurried to him and touched his arm, stopping him. "I'm sorry, Chad." She gazed into his eyes. "I spoke without think-ing."

"Maybe you're right. Maybe I am too old to learn readin'. Good night, Libby."

She watched him walk to the corrals. He stole a glance. She was still standing there in the yard when he stepped into the dark barn. He was a fool — an old fool, and didn't someone once say those were the worst kind of fool?

CHAPTER 10

Chad beat the sun to breakfast the next morning and he was riding away from the ranch even as the first blush of pink washed the eastern plains. A breeze held the promise of rain. Clouds moved down from the north, dark in the dawn light, churning and flashing.

A cold rain sweeping eastward edged past Chad. He pulled on a slicker as he rode. When he arrived at Thunder Canyon, the sky had cleared and men were already busy atop the crest of the dam. Chad turned onto a trail, putting the noise of the construction at his back. It was peaceful down in the chilled canyon along the stream. Here he could put troubles out of mind. Here he was in control of his life, and reading and writing belonged to another world. Here he did not need to think of anything but cow-boying — here he was at peace.

Passing the side canyon he wondered if

Cobsworth was chipping away at the rocky tomb that held the skull. Chad forcefully put the thought out of mind. His job was to find Rocking S cows and herd them safely out of the canyon, not to worry about the bone digger.

Further up the stream he spotted a yearling grazing a patch of bunch grass. Chad crossed the water and got it moving up the stream with him. A while later he spied another, and by noon he'd worked his way to the canyon's head and managed to fix himself up a pretty herd of three animals. He turned back downstream.

When the side canyon drew near, Chad kept his view straight ahead, his mind on the job at hand. The animals moved easily, almost as if they knew at the end of this trek there was grass aplenty waiting them. Chad rode past the canyon and would have kept going if at that instant the boom of a rifle shot hadn't tumbled out of the gap and brought Chad's head about with a start. It wasn't Cobsworth's rifle. That had been a little .22. He reined as the crack of a second shot came from the break.

Chad put spurs to his horse and scrambled up into the broken ground, up the trickle of water. Two more shots followed, louder now. He reined to a stop at Cobsworth's campsite. At the same time the crack of the rifle and a puff of gun smoke pointed out the gunman's location high up on the canyon's rim, behind some rocks. Chad swung his Sharps toward the smoke. The roar of the big fifty filled the narrow ravine, his bullet sending chips of stone flying. There was a blur of movement and by time Chad had reloaded, the gunman had fled.

"Cobsworth!"

Chad surveyed the ravine but the bone digger was nowhere to be seen. A cook fire smoldered and the horse and mule were properly tethered in the shade, watching nervously. Something caught his eye. He frowned. It was a shoe poking out from behind a boulder. Chad stalked around it and there was the bone digger, face down, head buried under his arms. Chad felt a pang of regret. There had been something likable about the fellow. It was too bad he came to this end.

The man stirred.

"Cobsworth? You alive?"

The bone digger unfolded his arms and rolled over, eyes stretched wide. "Don't shoot!"

"You ain't shot already?"

"No, I am not — not yet."

Chad let out a long breath. "Then crawl

out from behind that rock."

Cobsworth scooted out and stood with his arms stretched to the sky.

"Now what are you doing?"

"Surrendering."

"Surrendering? What for?" In spite of his initial relief, Chad was growing irritated with the bone digger.

He shrugged. "So you don't shoot me, of course." And it sounded as if Cobsworth was growing a bit peeved as well.

"You think it was me up there?" Chad was both hurt and angry, and he wanted to knock the bone digger from here to next Sunday, but he restrained himself.

Cobsworth nodded and his voice squeaked. "You wanted me to leave."

Ignoring his better judgment, Chad hauled back and sent Cobsworth sprawling. "If'n that was me up there you wouldn't be sitting there wiping that blood from your lip. I gave you three weeks and that's what you got, buster. If'n I wanted you out of here sooner I'd just pick you up and throw you out." He drew in a breath and turned back toward his horse. Why had he even cared? The bone digger wasn't worth it.

"You mean it wasn't you?" Cobsworth stood, pressing a handkerchief to his mouth.

"That's right, Swifty." Chad shoved his

rifle into its scabbard and stepped into the stirrup.

"Wait. Don't go. Who would want to kill me?"

Chad studied him from atop his horse then peered back at the rock that had hidden the ambusher. "Off hand, I'd say no one."

Cobsworth stared at him, a bewildered look in his eyes, then he looked at the remains of his fire, bent for a tin cup in the sand and spilled dirt from it. "Then I leaped for cover for no good reason." He sighed and looked at the cup.

"Can't say I wouldn't have done the same, Mr. Cobsworth."

The bone digger shook the pot. "Sounds like at least two cups left in here."

His way of making peace, and Chad dismounted. It was hard to stay mad at the dandy for very long. "Reckon the least I can do is help you drink it."

Cobsworth grinned and winced at the same time, found another cup among his gear and carefully divided the coffee between them. "You know, that wasn't very sporting of you, hitting a man when he wasn't expecting it. The honorable way of fisticuffs is for two men to square off face-to-face."

Chad laughed. "Whal, Cobsworth, out here the Marquis of Queensberry rules don't apply. Besides, what do you know about proper fisticuffs? You're a bone digger."

Cobsworth glanced up, a thin-line smile shaping his lips. "Williamstown Amateur Pugilist Society. Eighteen sixty through sixty-three."

"Really? You a fighter?"

Cobsworth struck a pose and wheeled his fist with first-class showmanship. "Division champion of sixty-three. Queensberry's rules hadn't arrive yet. Back then we fought under the old London Prize Ring Rules. Bare fists no holds barred. Ouch!"

Chad laughed again. "Could have fooled me."

Cobsworth's bright smile faded and he slumped out of his pose. "I was a different man back then." He sighed. "Those days are behind me, yet sometimes I think on them wistfully."

"Yep, know what you mean, Cobsworth." He glanced to the bone digger's meager pile of grub. "Getting kinda low on supplies, aren't you?"

"That's an understatement. But with only three weeks' time allotted to me, I don't have any extra to spend going into town."

"Any meat left?"

Cobsworth shrugged. "A little bacon and some jerked beef. It'll last." He pointed at a slim .22 rifle leaning against the gnarled bole of a juniper. "I'll hunt some rabbits later."

"You won't find much down here. Best to hunt 'em up on the flats."

"Further up this canyon is a trail that goes to the top. Looks like it might have been used by Indians many years ago."

Chad nodded. "Likely. They used to gather flint down in these canyons."

Cobsworth sipped his coffee carefully, avoiding the swollen lip. Chad regretted hitting him, but it seemed a good idea at the time. Cobsworth looked to the ridgeline. "What makes you think he wasn't trying to kill me?"

"Were you sitting here drinking coffee when he shot at you?"

"Yes. This very spot."

Chad's view hitched toward the rim of the canyon. "It's not a hundred feet to there. That fellow would have had to be near blind not to have hit you, Mr. Cobsworth."

He looked at Chad. "What are you suggesting?"

"Someone wants you gone, not dead."

"Who? Why? No one knows I'm here."

"McSween and his daughter know."

"Would they . . . ?"

Chad shook his head. "If'n McSween wanted you out of here he'd pick you up by the scruff and throw you out, and there wouldn't be a thing you could do to stop him. He's not a back-shooter."

Cobsworth's view grew distant. "The only other person who knows my location is . . . but, no, that's impossible." He shook his head as if to cast off the thought.

"What other person?"

"No one. I was just thinking out loud."

Chad sipped some coffee, which tasted pretty good. "My advice for you is to pay more attention to your back side from here on out, Mr. Cobsworth."

Cobsworth looked to the skull, mostly chipped free from its rocky grave. "That has my full attention."

"And that will get you killed."

"Maybe so." His voice trailed off.

"You really got an itch for them bones, don't you?"

Cobsworth pulled his eyes back to Chad's face. "And that seems a strange occupation to you?"

"Whal, to be straight-up honest, Mr. Cobsworth, yes."

"I don't have any excuse for myself," he

answered with a note of amusement in his voice. "I happen to be infatuated with the past — the far past, long before man was around to record it with pen and ink. That bone is a clue to the past, a tangible link to a bygone age. It may very well turn out to be an important piece in a puzzle that will eventually solve a very big mystery. Maybe not in my lifetime, maybe a hundred years from now. Someday those bones will live again in a museum where scientists can touch and measure and ponder them."

"Sounds mighty high-minded."

Cobsworth smirked and winced at the same time. His lip had stopped bleeding but it hurt. "I wish it was so, Chad. But high-minded it isn't — at least not yet. Paleontology is a young science and for now it seems to strictly be a race to see which man can find the most bones and send them back east as fast as an express train can carry them. I wonder how much we're losing in our haste?"

"If you say so. I don't know enough about what you just said to judge by. Shoot, I can't read but a handful of words as it is. Just enough to get through the paperwork I need to get writ up for the ranch."

"That's right. We were going to teach you to read. I'd forgotten."

Chad shook his head feeling the sting of Libby's words again. "I'm too old. And anyway, what does an old wrangler need with reading?"

"Nonsense. A man is never too old to learn to read. And a wrangler needs to know how just as anyone — to know what newspapers have to tell you, or store signs, or Holy Scriptures, or simply to enjoy reading books."

"Books? You mean ones like that one called Don Coyote?"

He stared a moment. "Don Coyote?" Then he laughed. "Yes, I suppose you could learn to read that one, although it is a rather challenging tome for a beginner. But, yes, of course, someday certainly you will be able to read Don Quixote, and hundreds of other books as well. You might even read a book on paleontology!"

"There's books writ on them bones?"

"Yes, indeed, and on a thousand other subjects — on just about anything you can think about."

A thought grabbed away his breath. "How about the stars?"

"Chad, there is literally a galaxy of books on astronomy — some going back hundreds of years."

He'd never heard of a galaxy of anything,

but it sounded like a number with a lot of aughts behind it. If he could read a book on stars, he could answer Eric's questions. All of them. A spark ignited somewhere inside him that lifted him from his narrow world and stood him upon a mountaintop where he spied away out on the horizon another world waiting to be explored. And the only tool in his kit bag that he needed to carry along on the trek was the ability to cipher the symbols on the page of a book. He didn't want to show his feelings to Cobsworth, didn't want to believe it could be a possibility in his life, didn't want to face the possibility that it would never happen. He hid his face momentarily behind the coffee cup, finished the last of it then handed the cup back to Cobsworth. He threw a rope about his emotions and snubbed it down tight. "I'll think on it some, Mr. Cobsworth."

"You do that Chad . . . but don't take too long. We only have three weeks."

Three weeks. It would take a sight longer than that to learn him to read. A stone settled in Chad's stomach as he stood. "I have animals I have to move out of the canyon." He went to his horse.

"See you again?"

He stepped up into his saddle. "Maybe."

He kept his tone even, neither a commitment nor a denial, but he knew the truth. Three weeks would not be enough time.

"Wait!" Cobsworth rose to his feet, a little off balance, like a newborn calf looking for its mamma. "What should I do if that person comes back?"

Chad considered a moment. "Say a quick prayer that he hasn't been practicing."

CHAPTER 11

The explosion came of a sudden, far away
at first, then rumbling like a train around a
bend in Thunder Canyon. Chad's horse
shied back and the cows began turning
nervous circles. Here and there loose rocks
clattered down into the canyon, and for a
brief moment everything seemed to be in
motion. It came and passed in two heart-
beats and the air grew horribly still as if it
had been a ghost that had passed through,
the foreboding silence broken only by a few
clattering pebbles sliding from the cliffs and
a great flock of ravens swarming above the
cottonwood trees like a black storm cloud.

Chad saw the brownish plume rising into
the clear sky and knew what it meant. The
dam! He kicked his horse into motion and
made a wide sweep, bringing the scattered
cows together then hurried them ahead. The
dam was still a half mile away and by the
time he rounded the last bend, the brown

cloud had mostly settled and the gaping hole that split McSween's dam down one side told him his hunch had been correct.

Chad rode over to the men gathered nearby, bunched up like a herd of cows. "How'd it happen?"

"A wagonload of dynamite went off — the whole thing, Chad," one of the men said.

"Anyone hurt?" Looking at the destruction he hoped against hope that no one had. The man's words soon shattered even that.

"At least three dead I know of. Don't know yet for sure. The Colonel took a head count then went to check on the damage. Corky's over there with Timbledee doctoring on a couple men who got in the way of the blast."

Chad rode to the chuck wagon, surveying the damage as he went. The bottom outlet was now a great chasm beneath a fresh blanket of settling dirt. A few men were over there examining the damage. He didn't see Harrison. He dismounted at the wagon and stood over two blanket-covered bodies. He pulled back the cover. Ross and Bicker. He covered them again and went over to where Corky and Timbledee were working. Their patients were Penrose, Berryman, Pickles and Stovill.

"How bad are they?"

Corky glanced up. "Chad. Didn't hear you come up. Don't know. Some just got banged up pretty bad."

Of the four, only Pickles was conscious, looking more dazed than hurt.

"How'd it happen?"

Timbledee, pressing a bloody cloth to Penrose's head, looked up at him. "Filbert and Stovill went into town this morning for the dynamite. When they got back they parked the wagon over there, near the bottom outlet. Stovill was bringing the papers over here when the wagon exploded. He was lucky he wasn't killed."

"What about Filbert?" Chad glanced about.

Corky frowned. "Terry was still with the wagon. I seen him there, sitting on the bench." He shook his head. "T'weren't enough of him left to find. Near as I figure it, Chad, Terry must have struck a match. Maybe lighting one of them cigars he all the time smokes."

Chad said, "Dynamite don't go off that way, Corky. It needs to be capped, and sealed cases of dynamite aren't capped."

"Don't you think I know that, Chad? I don't know what happened and I've had my hands full here to try and figure it out."

Timbledee said, "Might have been a bad

batch. Sometimes dynamite leaches nitro-glycerin. When that happens, even a nudge can set it off."

Chad had heard of that happening, but it didn't seem likely with fresh explosives. There had to be another reason but like Corky, he had more immediate problems to think about. "Have you sent for Doctor Bleaker?"

Corky shook his head. "Haven't had time yet."

Chad glanced back at the men. "Canfield."

"Yeah, boss?"

"Ride into Cañon and fetch the doc."

"Right, boss."

"Tell him to meet us at the bunkhouse. Some of you men fix a bed of blankets in those buckboards. Let's get these four back to the ranch." He turned back to Timbledee. "Where's Harrison?"

"Last I saw of him, he was surveying the damages."

Surveying damages? With injured men needing help? Chad knew a sudden surge of anger. He threw a fast rope on it and called out to another man, "Blake! Find that blue-belly colonel and bring him to me. Tell him we have injured men here and his precious dam can damn well wait."

"My pleasure, Chad." Blake gave a big grin as if he'd been waiting for an opportunity to say something like that to Harrison.

Two buckboards were brought over and the men carefully lifted onto them. As Stovill was being moved, something fluttered from his vest pocket. Chad snatched up the folded piece of paper and immediately recognized the fancy scroll decoration along the top edge and the bold letters. THE PACIFIC TELEGRAPH COMPANY. He knew the words the letters spelled out because he'd seen them before, but the words scrawled in a flowing script were a meaningless jumble.

"All ready to go, Chad," Corky said.

Chad stuck the telegram into his pocket and checked on the men in the wagon beds. It worried him mightily that so far only Pickles was conscious. There was lots of blood soaking through the hastily applied bandages, but Chad had a feeling that the injuries were worse than even the bloody bandages made them seem. He swung up onto his saddle and took one last look at the ruined dam. Just then Colonel Harrison strolled out of the shattered bottom outlet wearing a scowl that Chad determined was a notch or two more sour than his usual disagreeable expression. Blake followed a few steps behind him, a cat-that-ate-the-mouse grin on his lips.

"You requested to see me, Mr. Larimer?" Harrison snapped.

"I did. Just thought you'd like to know we have injured men here, and some who weren't so lucky."

"Is that all? I know we have casualties. Three dead and four wounded." Harrison's face remained hard. Chad imagined death and injury were old saddle pals of his. A man in his line of work had seen a lot of those two villains, and they moved him not at all now.

"Casualties? Need I remind you, Colonel, we are not fighting a war here."

Harrison exhaled an impatient breath. "Is this all you wanted to tell me?"

"No, it's not. Mr. McSween is going to want to hear an explanation and you're the one who's gonna give it. So, mount up."

"Me? See here, Larimer. I give the orders . . ." His words cut short and his eyes shifted to Chad's holstered revolver where Chad now rested his hand on the dark grips.

Chad hadn't meant it as a threat. It had been a mostly unconscious movement, but now that he'd done it and seen Harrison's reaction to it, he let his hand remain so as not to discourage Harrison from imagining the worse. "Mr. Harrison. You will accompany me now. Either sitting on your saddle or hog-tied and slung over it, kicking and screaming if you like. Your choice."

Harrison's nostrils flared and Chad could see Harrison was deliberating calling Chad's bluff. Chad half hoped the colonel would. In the end, Harrison spun away on his heels and strode across the bottom of the canyon to where the horses were picketed. In a couple minutes, he had his McClellen saddle cinched tight and rode to the wagons in a stiff fashion, the result of too many turns around a parade ground, Chad mused.

"Let's be off, then," Harrison said coolly. "My men will need me back here soon if I'm to get the dam repaired."

"You'll be back soon enough, Colonel, and *your* men will still be here." Chad looked to Blake. "There are three cows on the other side of the dam. Bring 'em around and run 'em out to Coal Creek with the others there."

"Yes, sir, Chad. It'll be right pleasant to be doing some fitting work for a change."

Chad knew what he meant. Shoveling dirt and taking orders from men like Harrison was not what men like Blake had signed on with McSween to do.

He got his little troop of buckboards and injured men moving. Not far along the trail, Colonel Harrison moved ahead, taking the point.

Old habits were hard to change.

CHAPTER 12

McSween lowered himself into his chair and for a while the only sound in the office was the rhythmic creak of him rocking back and forth in it. Libby gave Chad a sideways glance, a fading smile upon her face. The somber mood had spread like a prairie fire as the news Chad had brought sunk in.

"They were good men," McSween said after a long moment ruminating on what he'd just been told. His wild, gray eyebrows dipped together cutting a V between his scowling eyes. "Bicker and Filbert been with us almost from the beginning, Ross nearly as long."

The cigar McSween had been smoking when Chad and Harrison had arrived rested in the groove of an ashtray, growing a long, gray cylinder of ash. McSween snatched it up, jamming it between his teeth. "And no one knows how it happened?" His voice was skeptical now, his eyes probing.

Chad said, "Timbledee suspects Filbert lit up a cigar while in the wagon."

"Poppycock. Only a fool would light a match sitting on five hundred pounds of dynamite, and Filbert wasn't a fool. And besides, you could build a bonfire under that stuff and it wouldn't explode."

"Perhaps a carton of faulty blasting caps?" Harrison suggested stiffly. Since arriving he'd ignored Chad.

McSween shifted his view to the colonel. "I've never heard of that happening but I suppose it's possible. Aren't the caps packaged separately from the dynamite?"

"Usually. But mistakes happen."

"Father, what difference does it make how it happened? This delay will cost us weeks. Maybe longer."

Her words wrenched Chad from his thoughts, which had been on the men, not the dam, or any delay the accident might have caused.

But she continued as if the men who had died were of no importance. "Colonel Harrison, how long will it take to repair the damage?"

Harrison pushed out his lower lip and gave Chad a withering scowl. "I knew that you would want to know. I was attempting to properly assess the damage when Mr.

Larimer detoured me from my job by insisting I accompany him immediately. I'd planned on making a proper survey before reporting to you, Mrs. Russman."

Libby's view narrowed toward Chad a moment. "I quite understand."

McSween said, "Best guess."

Harrison flashed a small smile and looked back at McSween. "The bottom drain is collapsed. I'll have to excavate it and rebuild it. That will mean disturbing the integrity of the clay core." He shook his head. "If we work double shifts, I can have the repair complete in two weeks, three at the most."

Libby said, "I declare, I don't want to see another summer like the last — so hot and dry, cattle suffering for lack of water."

McSween grunted and shifted his view back to Harrison. "Two weeks?"

"Three at the outmost, if the men put their backs to it."

"We're already pushing them hard," McSween countered.

"I'll push them harder," Harrison said.

McSween looked worried. Chad knew what he was thinking. He had good men working on the dam and they had already given more than he had a right to ask. How much farther might he push them? He looked at Chad and must have seen Chad's concern. "What do you think about this?"

Chad was a little startled to be suddenly included. Where the dam was concerned, Harrison was the trail boss. Chad felt Libby's view shift toward him and it seemed like she was waiting, as if his answer was some kind of test of his loyalty. "You got good men out there and they're working hard for the colonel. You might push and get a little more out of them, and you might drive them off too. Maybe we ought to hire on a few more hands until we get back on track?"

McSween frowned, glancing distractedly about the room as if hoping to find an answer to the problem there. When his eyes came to rest upon the old Hawken rifle leaning in the corner a glimmer of a smile came to his lips. Was he thinking about a simpler time? He looked back and the smile was gone. "We're working short as it is and I can't afford to pull any more of my men away from their jobs here on the ranch. I can't afford to hire on more either so we'll have to do with what we got."

Chad said, "Then maybe we just forget finishing the dam this year. We still have cows on the high pastures that need to be brought down before the snows come."

"Chadwick!" Libby's eyes flamed. "I

declare, you don't care anything about Father and me! You know how important this project is." Her voice lowered, holding both a warning and a veiled enticement, "And it should be important to you too." She left the rest unspoken but the carrot at the end of her stick was plain. If he played his cards right he could have her, and with her came the ranch. Another time it might have tempted him. Tonight he was in no mood to play her games.

"Libby!" McSween said, rising to his feet and planting his fists upon the desktop.

She stiffened, cast Chad a warning glare then whirled around and left the room, slamming the door behind her.

McSween drew in a ragged breath. "Headstrong woman." The corners of his mouth hitched up a little. "Afraid that didn't come from her mother's side of the family."

Chad said nothing, but he was aware that something had changed inside him. It had been coming for some time now, but only recently had it grown into a conscious thought. He'd known Libby since she was a girl, knew the ranch had always been as important to her as it had to McSween himself, but for her it was somehow different. Where McSween was determined, Libby was ruthless. Chad wondered why it had taken so long for him to see that.

"What about my men?" Harrison demanded.

Chad stiffened and said to McSween, "If we don't start moving cattle down to winter pasture, it could be a bigger loss than the drought."

McSween was torn. He held devils by the tail in both hands, and letting go of either would have bad results. "Take what men you need, Colonel," he said.

There was a flash of victory in Harrison's eyes. "Good. I'll be off then. The sooner we get started the sooner we'll be back on schedule." He turned with a military snap and strode out of the room.

McSween looked at Chad. "You don't approve."

"Since when did you need my approval? It's your ranch, your men, your animals. I don't pay the wages, you do."

"But if it were your ranch . . . your men?"

"I'd not risk an early snowstorm trapping a thousand head of my beef up in the mountains where there'd be no food."

McSween leaned back in his chair and struck a match, putting it to a fresh cigar. "I'm having difficulty recalling the last time we disagreed on anything concerning the Rocking S, Chad. What's bothering you?

137

Certainly not that childish display Libby threw?"

Libby was part of it, but he didn't want to speak of it now. "I don't like Harrison. I don't like his overbearing attitude. He's not commanding soldiers out there. They're wranglers. They're good at what they do, and they deserve better treatment."

"Hum." McSween tugged thoughtfully at his beard. "And nothing else?"

There was something else, but until just then it had been only a vague notion, an itch he couldn't quite reach to scratch. Now, suddenly, he realized what the itch was. "I'm worried about Cobsworth. Someone hereabouts has decided he'd make a good target."

McSween's eyebrows shot up. "I thought that bone digger might have something to do with it. Bushwhacked? Was he hurt?"

"No."

"Good. Don't need any unnecessary killings on my land."

"I don't think the gunman intended to kill him. Only put a scare into him. Maybe run him off."

McSween pursed his lips, studying Chad. "You suggesting I had anything to do with it?"

Chad laughed. "Bushwhacking ain't your

style, C. L. I'm inclined to believe it's not someone from the Rocking S but someone who knows what he's found, knows it's important and wants to keep Cobsworth from finishing his work."

"Ridiculous! Who'd give a wooden nickel about a pile of old bones?"

"I thought that too until he told me bones like what he found are worth a passel of honor and money to some folks back east. He's worried someone might try to steal them from him, someone named Marsh."

"Marsh? I've read something of the man. Another bone digger. I'll say it again, Chad, it's downright strange to get so wrapped up with a pile of bones — more than strange, it's wrong!" McSween's eyes narrowed. "I would not have been as generous as you, but since you've given him three weeks, I will abide by that, however, come the end of the month he'll be out of Thunder Canyon."

"He's not hurting anything, C. L. Give him the few extra weeks it's gonna take to get the dam repaired."

"No. He's already caused trouble. I don't need bushwhackers on my land. I don't need anything more to delay the completion of that dam. Is that understood?" McSween's ice-blue eyes could have stopped a grizzly cold in its tracks and Chad felt his spine stiffen in response.

The door opened and Libby breezed in like a cool wind, her skirt rustling across the floor like dried autumn leaves. She moved past Chad without a glance. McSween shifted his gaze toward her as she stopped in front of his desk. "Doctor Bleaker has arrived, Father."

"Good. Get him over to the bunkhouse right away. Chad and I will be along shortly."

Libby nodded and turned away, her eyes flashing past Chad as if he wasn't even in the room, and the door closed quietly behind her.

McSween let go of a long breath and whatever tension there had been between the two men had evaporated with Libby's news. McSween leaned back in his chair again. "Go see to Bleaker," he said fingering the papers on his desk. "I'll be along in a few minutes."

Chad just stood there.

McSween looked up at him. "You going to buck me on this too?"

"I've always considered you a reasonable man, C. L. But you're not acting reasonable now."

"As you said just a moment ago. It's my

ranch, I pay the wages. Far as I'm concerned this case is closed." He said it in a tone of voice Chad reckoned McSween had used in his younger days teaching law at Harvard. Only, Chad was not one of his students and the matter was far from closed far as he was concerned.

He left McSween there, followed the hallway to the parlor and was heading out the door when Libby called to him. He stopped, hearing the dry-leaf rustle come up behind him. He turned. Her eyes had changed, no longer spitting sparks now but slate hard and calculating.

"I declare, Chad, I don't understand your behavior. Father's treated you as a son all these years."

He spoke in a level voice, keeping his anger from coming out in his words. "Even fathers and sons disagree, Libby."

"There can be no disagreement where the Rocking S is concerned." Her hard eyes narrowed. "You never have in the past."

It was true. He'd always gone along with everything McSween had ever wanted to do. He'd rarely question any of McSween's decisions. It has always been the ranch and nothing else had much mattered. His life, he realized, had been given over to McSween, Libby, and the Rocking S.

Libby moved closer to him. "The Rocking S should be as important to you as it is to him." Her voice softened, losing its menace. "Someday it could all belong to you if . . ." She left the rest unspoken and reached up to kiss him.

He recoiled from her touch. There was no love in her lips. It was an act, a way to keep him under her spell, under her controlling wishes.

She backed away, her searching eyes confused. "You've changed."

"Have I? Maybe it's that I'm realizing that the sun doesn't rise and set just to please the whims of Libby McSween Russman, or C. L. for that matter."

He left her standing in the open doorway, hurried down the porch steps and headed toward the bunkhouse.

CHAPTER 13

"Chad! Chad!" Eric called to him.

Chad halted his determined strides and came about as the boy hurried across the yard.

"Hi, Chad. Gosh, haven't seen you in days." Eric's wide smile was warm enough to melt an iceberg and Chad felt his own bitterness thaw under its glow.

He tousled the boy's hair. "Just getting home from school?" He nodded at the books tucked under Eric's arm.

"Yep. That's Doc Bleaker's rig, ain't it? Someone get hurt?"

"Had an accident down by your grandpa's dam."

Eric's face turned concerned. "Bad accident?"

Chad nodded grimly, feeling a heaviness in his chest. "Three good men killed. Another four hurt. Doc's with them now."

"Gosh. What happened?"

"Someone got careless around a wagon-load of dynamite."

"Gosh." His brown eyes widened.

"I'm on my way to check on them now."

Eric fell in step beside him.

"Howdy, Chad," Ben Pickles said from his bunk where he lay when Chad and Eric entered. "I've been thinking I needed a vacation. Never planned on taking it this way." Pickles grinned.

"Always figured you for a goldbricker, Ben."

Stovill looked over from his bunk and smiled weakly and didn't say anything.

Doc Bleaker looked grim.

"Pretty bad, Doc?"

"Pickles has some bumps and bruises. Stovill, a mild concussion. And Penrose over there, he'll be wearing his arm in a sling the next four months. He's asleep now. I gave him a pretty strong dose of laudanum to kill the pain. It's Berryman here that I'm worried about." The corners of Doc Bleaker's mouth dipped in a frown. "Hasn't regained consciousness yet." Bleaker lifted one of Berryman's eyelids and studied the eye a moment. Even Chad could see there was no reaction to the light in the wide pupil.

"This is very serious. The flash must have

caught him full in the eyes. And he has a severe concussion."

"Can you do anything for him, Doc?"

"I don't know. I'll have to dig through my medical books and hope to find an answer. In the meantime, I want to take him to my house where I have better facilities." He grimaced. "That might not be enough. I'm not set up to be a hospital. Berryman will be better off in Colorado Springs, or even Denver."

Chad shook his head. "That's a long way to move him."

"I agree. We'll take him to my place first where I can keep a close eye on him." He looked up at Chad. "In the end, it comes down to how strong he is . . . and whatever help he might get from the Almighty."

"It always does," Chad agreed ruefully. "I'll get a buckboard ready."

Eric said, "I can do that. I'll tell Grandpa."

"Thanks, pard." Eric left and Chad moved to Stovill's bunk. "What happened out there?"

Stovill's left eye was swollen and a layer of hide had been scraped from his cheek on the same side. Stovill gave a little shrug, favoring his left shoulder. "I don't know, Chad. When we got back from town, I left Terry holding the wagon while I went off to

145

find Harrison, to see where he wanted us to unload the dynamite. Next thing I knew, a pile driver slammed me from behind." He rotated his arm and winced. "I must have been thrown in the air. Don't remember though, but I have a pretty good idea what side I landed on."

"And you have no idea how it happened?"

He frowned and shook his head upon his pillow. "Wish I could help, Chad. Sorry."

Eric plopped himself down next to Chad on the top step of Chad's little cottage. "Grandpa is really upset, isn't he?"

Across the way, Berryman was being carried out of the bunkhouse on a stretcher. The men moved slowly, carefully to the back of the buckboard and slid the stretcher into the wagon bed, latching the tailgate. Doc Bleaker said something to McSween then walked toward his little buggy.

"I reckon he has a right to be mad. Mad enough to order Pickles and Stovill back to the work site tomorrow even though Doc recommended a couple days' rest for both of 'em."

"You think he shouldn't have, Chad?"

Chad shrugged. "I'm inclined to think Doc Bleaker knows a mite more about this matter than your grandpa. That dam is a burr under his saddle. With winter coming on and time running out, he's gotten jumpy as a frog in a coyote patch."

Eric watched Doc Bleaker heading toward his rig. "Why, Chad?"

"You grandpa's got big stakes riding on all that water he expects to corral in Thunder Canyon. When you get a little older, you'll understand."

"I don't know as I'll ever understand grownups, Chad."

Chad gave a short laugh. "It sorta comes natural . . . when you get old." The sky was darkening with the coming evening and suddenly Chad was thinking about Cobsworth. It would already be mostly dark in that side canyon where he was patiently chipping away at the rock. Another lonely night with only old bones and the ghost of a long-dead critter to keep him company. Chad thought about that giant skull. It alone would be about all a single mule could carry. It would take a dozen trips back and forth to move all those bones out of the canyon and to safety. The place would be under thirty feet of water before the task was done. All that work for naught.

"Why you frowning, Chad?"

He hadn't realized that he was. "Just pondering a few things, Eric. You ever hear of a critter called a dinosawer?"

"Don't recall, Chad. What's a dinosawer?"

"Whal, let me tell you about them. A dinosawer is a critter what used to live right out there where your grandpa's beeves are grazing now, only, it weren't like no critter you ever did lay eyes on afore. No sir. Ever see an elephant?"

"Course I seen one, Chad. Seen it at a circus once."

"Whal, the tallest elephant that ever growed wouldn't but reach to a dinosawer knee bone. The critters were as long as a bunkhouse from nose to the end of their long tail."

Eric gave Chad a skeptical look. "Shoot, you can't devil me with a tale like that. I ain't some greenhorn."

"I ain't greening you, son. It's true."

"If them dinosawer critters do live around these parts, how come I ain't ever seen me one?"

"Cause they're all dead, all gone now. Not a single one left in the whole wide world. But at one time there was wonderful herds of 'em."

"Who killed them?"

Chad rolled his shoulder. "Don't rightly know. Comanches, I suspect."

"I ain't never heard no Indian tales about

148

it. How do you know about them?"

"I know a man who's found their bones."

"Oh, you mean that bone digger camped out in Thunder Canyon." Eric sounded disappointed.

"How'd you hear about him?"

"Grandpa told of him at dinner last night. Said he was a grave robber and that were a dangerous thing to be. Said they was no better than rustlers. Both were thieves only their victims were different."

"We both know your grandpa's a real smart man, Eric, but he doesn't know about everything. Trouble is, he spent too many years hobnobbing with the Injuns, sitting around their campfires listening to their superstitions. It's made him skittish, that's all."

Eric laughed. "Don't say that to his face, Chad."

"Already did."

"Whoo-ee, and he didn't bite your head off?"

"Nope. In fact, he sorta agreed with me . . . sorta. Still didn't change his mind on the matter."

The buckboard rolled up alongside Doc Bleaker's buggy and together they started away from the house.

"How come the bone digger knows so

much about these dinosawer critters?"

Bleaker and the buckboard passed under the Rocking S shingle into the growing dusk. "He's what you call a pay-lee-o-tologist. It's his job to know about bones just like it's my job to know about cows. He studied on 'em in school, read a book or two about 'em too."

"Really?"

"Right 'nough, pard. Books'll tell a fellow all he needs to know 'bout old bones and the sort of critter they come from. And books can teach him how to read them bones like your grandpa can read an Injun trail." The words came out with conviction, but inside they rang hollow and ripped opened a painful wound.

"Do you know how to read bones, Chad?" Eric's eyes were wide with awe and Chad felt obliged not to disappoint the boy.

"Whal, I reckon I can some. Like them bones Cobsworth found in Thunder Canyon. Why, right off I know'd they weren't from any critter around these parts — leastwise, not any still breathing God's own sweet air. I studied 'em some and figured they was from a critter long dead and buried. Pay-lee-o-tologists call them 'extinct.' I looked them bones over and knew Cobsworth had found himself a brand-new critter what ain't ever been seen afore. Pay-lee-o-tologists call 'em new 'species.' "

"Really, Chad?"

Chad winced, his chest tightening. "Really. Ask your teacher about species. He's most likely read a book or two on the matter."

"What kind of species was it, Chad?"

His mind went blank. Cobsworth had a name for it but try as he might, Chad couldn't remember it. He hesitated, pushing out his lower lip in a contemplative way, stalling for time. "Whal, I reckon it don't have no name yet seeing as it's a new species." Then something Cobsworth had said came to him. "But it looks to be a second cousin to another extinct critter what's called a dippi-o-docus." The word sounded right — close enough for a lie that was growing uncomfortably out of hand.

Eric looked up at him with wonderment and Chad felt lower than a bucket down a well. Why had he done it? He'd never lied to Eric, and even teasing he always let the truth be known — eventually. But that wasn't going to be the case this time. He couldn't stand to see the fire die from Eric's eyes, couldn't bear to be made to feel like a simpleton who knew nothing more than how to wrangle cows. Chad couldn't explain it. Something had come over him when Eric had turned those eyes of admiration on him. It was a look the boy reserved for special things and of recent it was missing when Chad spoke of cowboying or Injun fighting.

Then Libby called for Eric from the house.

"Coming, Ma." Eric stood. "Gotta go, Chad. Dinnertime. See ya later." He hopped off the step and hurried across the yard. Libby kept her view averted, purposefully avoiding looking over to where Chad sat on the top step. She seemed a cold stone, maybe because he'd seen a side of her today he'd not noticed before. His heart grew a lump of discontentment the size of — of a dippi-o-docus — as he watched Eric trot off. Something had changed and he couldn't put a word to the feeling.

With a grimace, he stood, glancing to the bunkhouse where McSween was just leaving, having heard Libby's call as well. Chad didn't want to confront McSween now and turned and scuffed into his little house.

CHAPTER 14

Chad looked at the book McSween had given him, hesitating at first to slip it into the saddlebag, about to toss it aside but then changing his mind. It wasn't too big or cumbersome to be a bother and maybe, just maybe . . .

A knock on the door pulled him from his thoughts.

Libby stood there when he pulled the door open. Her face radiant and lovely as ever. Her eyes soft, yet bright. She hugged a sweater about her shoulders, her hair pulled back from her face and held in place with ribbons. A pleasant aroma enveloped her, not overpowering, just subtle enough to tease a man, to make him wonder whether or not his nose was playing tricks on him.

She waited expectantly. He was surprised to see her there after the unpleasantness earlier. When he didn't speak right away she said, "May I come in?"

His brain seemed to have momentarily jumped track. He recovered and stepped aside for her. She entered, turned and looked at him appraisingly. "Are you going somewhere?" Her eye lowered to the saddlebags in his hand.

He hung them over the back of a chair. "I'm riding to Thunder Canyon in the morning."

Her view moved away from him, circled the sparse room with its worn furniture. "We missed you at dinner this evening." She sat upon the corner of the bed and smoothed the long folds of her skirt without looking up at him.

"I don't recall being invited."

Her view shot up, narrowing. "Since when do you require a special invitation, Chadwick?"

He let go of a long breath. "Is that why you're here tonight, or is there something else you want to talk to me about?"

The glint of blue anger passed from her eyes, replaced with a look he'd seen before. His heart began to beat a little faster.

She patted the bed next to her. "Sit by me, Chad."

He knew the game. She had let her hold on him slip earlier today and now she wanted it back. It would have been easy to give in tonight, but this isn't what he wanted from her — not now at least. A strained moment passed. "All right, don't." She looked away from him, started to say something and stopped, changing her mind. "Am I that obvious?"

"Yes, ma'am, you are."

She looked away, folded her hands on her lap and looked down at them. It was a simple gesture but the way she did it was designed to make a man feel horribly strong and conquering. He might have even fallen for it too, except he knew Libby well enough to know she was acting again. "I thought that after what happened, you'd at least want to apologize to me" — she looked up with large liquid blue eyes — "to make up."

He gave a short laugh. He hadn't meant to do it. It was just that her game was so plainly transparent again.

Libby's face went hard. "So, that's the way you feel. I see I've wasted my time coming here. I declare Chadwick Larimer, I don't understand why you are doing this to me . . . to yourself. You seem intent on throwing away any chance to have this ranch — to have . . ." She bit back her words.

In spite of himself, he felt the anger welling again. "But the ranch doesn't come without a price, does it, Libby? The cost is keeping Libby McSween Russman happy at all costs."

"Is there something awful about that?" She tossed her head. "Do you blame me?"

"Whatever happened to you in the past was of your own making. Ten years ago I was right here for you. You made your choice. It was pretty clear I wasn't good enough for you then. What's changed now? Is it because people talk and they say cruel things? That you drove Gary Russman into the arms of other women?"

She lurched to her feet and slapped him. "I hate you."

The sting in his face was small compared to the rip in his heart. "Did you ever love me? Or am I only a way out of the muck Gary pulled you through? A shoulder to cry on? Was I ever any more than that to you, Libby?"

"Why did I even try? I should have known I couldn't have reasoned with a . . . with an unlearned cowboy."

Her brutal words hurt more than the slap on the face or the ache in his heart. They stopped him in his tracks, the pain from them stunning him into silence.

She pulled the door open then turned back to him. "You've not heard the last of this, Chadwick Larimer!" The door slammed behind her.

Through the window he watched her rush down the steps and stomp toward the house. Then she stopped, hesitating only a moment before swinging around and marching toward the bunkhouse. He grimaced. Libby was wasting no time. She'd lost one shoulder to cry on and needed another. Stovill would be the likely recipient.

An emptiness filled him, yet, as he turned away from the window an indefinite feeling of relief seemed to fill the hollow place in his chest. Any romantic feeling toward Libby had left him earlier that afternoon when he'd finally seen past the beauty to the cold, selfish woman who had revealed herself in C. L.'s office. Still, the two of them had been friends a lot of years and it was a bitter sadness to see it come to an end.

The sun was barely in the sky when Chad rode down into camp in Thunder Canyon next morning. Corky Rye had breakfast cooking and the wonderful aroma of frying ham and scrambled eggs drew Chad over to where some of the men were already filling their plates.

"Better hurry, Chad, or you'll pull up at

the end of the line," Corky said, grinning like a man who loved doing what he was doing.

When his turn came, Corky filled Chad's plate and said, "How's them four men we sent back with you?"

He told him what Doc Bleaker had said.

Corky frowned and gave a snort. "Blind. Them's sure sour apples for Berryman. Leastwise, the others got off easy. You say Stovill and Pickles will be back to work today? Humph, would have expected Mr. McSween to at least let 'em rest up a day or two."

"Doc Bleaker tried to talk him into it."

Corky shook his head. "He flat out said no?"

"Said he needed every man he's got to fix the damage. Not sure what's burring him, Corky. I know the dam is important, but so are his men — and his cattle. We're running late on the fall roundup. He'll have worse problems if'n he don't get those cows down to winter grass."

"It's called being single-minded."

Chad nodded in solemn agreement. "I'm headed back into the canyon."

"More beeves to round up?"

"Something like that. Can you fix me up a couple sacks of grub, if you have any to spare, and some coffee too."

Corky looked surprised. "You figuring on stayin' up there a while?"

"Never can tell, Corky."

"We got plenty of food. Mr. McSween might work us like coolies, but he does take care of our bellies."

Chad grinned. "I won't tell him you said that. And thanks, I'll take whatever you can spare."

Stovill and Pickles rode into camp. Pickles climbed stiffly off his horse, and Stovill lowered himself to the ground giving a muffled groan. They tied their horses to the picket line and walked over like two old men.

"Got any grub left, Corky?" Stovill asked.

"Still hot in the skillet."

He look over to Chad. "You're here bright and early, Chad."

Something in the way he said it made Chad wary. How long had Libby spoken with Stovill last night? Had she told him about Cobsworth? Maybe he was reading too much into it, imagining that he'd heard something in Stovill's voice that hadn't been there. "Got work to do," he said flatly.

Stovill grinned and took a plate of food from Corky and carried it over to where some other men sat eating.

Chad ate by himself, and by the time he'd finished Corky had gathered together enough grub to fill two flour sacks. Stovill watched from where he ate, and when Chad tied the bags to his saddle, Stovill stood and carried his tin cup to the coffeepot hanging nearby, over a bank of coals. "What's that you got there, Chad? Extra food?" He grinned.

Chad swung up onto his saddle and peered down at Stovill. "I'm right pleased to see the explosion did no permanent damage, Alex."

"Just some bumps and bruises. Too bad about Terry, isn't it? Well, it was a fast way to die — a good way to die." Stovill smiled up at him.

Chad had that wary feeling again. "I reckon, if any way of dying can be called good."

"I always say quick is better than slow."

"Suppose so. You were pretty lucky, Alex. Better watch your step, though. Next time might not go so well for you."

"I appreciate the concern, Chad, but I don't plan for there to be a next time."

"No one ever does."

"You needn't worry about me. I'm brimming over with luck."

"Like a brand-new shiny copper penny,

160

huh?" Chad grinned and clucked his horse ahead. Stovill's cocksure confidence was annoying. Chad put the man out of mind.

As he neared the dam he slowed to examine the ragged gash where the bottom drain had been and he thought of Terry Filbert. He'd known Terry a long time, and seemed to recall now how Terry always considered himself lucky, too. Chad shook his head, a rueful smile shaping his lips. In the end, Terry's luck ran out, just like it does for every man . . . eventually.

CHAPTER 15

A brisk wind had begun to blow by the time Chad reached the narrow side canyon where Cobsworth had found his dinosawer. Chad reined his horse toward the tall slit of an opening noting how the aspen trees stood stark and bare against the bright blue sky. The marshy ground along the stream held the strong odor of decaying leaves, bitter yet pleasant. An earthy, familiar smell. It was a reminder that winter was near. Sudden concern brought a tightness to his lips. The cows still in the high country were a constant worry now.

Chad let his horse pick its own way up the rocky ravine. When they came around the shoulder of rock, Cobsworth turned, hearing the horse's hooves scraping.

"Chad, come over here." He waved excitedly.

Chad slipped out of his saddle and climbed the slope where Cobsworth was kneeling over a pile of bones. The huge skull had been freed from its rocky grave and it rested upon the tarpaulin with a bunch of other bones. Cobsworth had a little broom in his hand, sweeping bits of dirt and rocks from the critter's empty eye socket.

"Look here, Chad." He pointed to a fat, round tooth, long as a man's hand is wide. It started out broad at the top and tapered down to a rounded point, a nearly perfect cone-shaped fang, Chad reckoned.

"It's a haplodont tooth! Just as I suspected!" He could hardly get a rope on his excitement.

"You don't say?" Chad tried to sound impressed, wondering how a tooth could make a grown man act like a boy being given his first rifle.

"All my information says this ought to be a diplodocus but the proportions are all wrong." Cobsworth conjured up an iron ruler from somewhere and laid it upon the skull. "See what I mean?"

Chad didn't see anything out of the ordinary.

"This distance from the anterior premaxillary along the suture to the anterior frontal bone is more than thirty percent longer than it should be for a diplodocus."

All that might as well have been spoken in

Chinese, but Chad nodded and looked impressed. "You don't say?"

"You know what that means?"

Chad took a stab at it. "You went and found yourself a new, whatchacallit, species?"

"That's exactly what it means!" Cobsworth nearly bowled himself over with excitement. "All my life I've hoped for a discovery like this, and now . . . now . . ." He couldn't go on. Nearly out of breath, he knelt there shaking his head. When he got up the strength to speak again his voice was hushed, like he was in church or at a funeral. "My name will go down in history." His head snapped around, eyes wide as saucers. "My name! My goodness, I almost forgot! I can name it whatever I want. Ha! What shall I call it? How about grandidentosaurus Cobsworthi? Ha-ha!"

"I reckon you can call it whatever you want to." Chad was enjoying seeing Cobsworth in such high spirits.

Cobsworth stared at the critter a long moment, the excitement slowly leaving his face. His head came around and there was suspicion in his voice. "What brings you back so soon? I didn't expect to see you until my reprieve was up."

Chad went to his horse and untied the

sacks. "Any more visits from the bush-whacker?"

"No. I have my twenty-two ready if I need it." He pointed to the little J. Stevens gallery rifle leaning against a nearby rock.

"Eaten anything lately?"

"I haven't had time to go hunting."

"Here." Chad tossed the sacks at Cobsworth's feet. "This will keep your belly full while you clean them bones."

Cobsworth opened one of them and lifted a questioning gaze to Chad. "Food?"

"And some coffee too. If'n you stoke up that cook fire there, we can have us a pot boiling in twenty minutes."

"I thought you wanted me out of here."

"Gave you to the end of the month, remember? If'n I wanted you out of here there's easier ways to be shuck of you than starving you out." Chad took the coffeepot and shook it near to his ear. "Besides, that food is for the both of us. I'll fetch some water."

"Both of us?"

Chad ambled to the stream, brushed aside some watercress growing in the seep and filled the pot. "For a while at least. Figured I'd take you up on that offer."

"Offer?"

Chad came back to the fire. "Reading."

He handed the pot to Cobsworth then went to his horse and fetched the book from his saddlebag. "I even brought along my own book to learn on."

Cobsworth's eyebrows hitched up and he took the book, turning it over, hefting it in his hand as if judging the weight of it. "I see you're not one to waste time beginning at the beginning."

"McSween give it to me. It's the only one I have. It'll work, won't it?"

Cobsworth laughed. "It'll work, Chad. We'll just make it work, won't we? At least it's not Don Quixote."

The bone digger's confidence filled Chad with hope. "I don't have Don Coyote . . . yet. Maybe next time. Now, how about that fire?"

Over the next three days Chad learned the names of more parts of a skeleton than a decent man had the right to know. During the mornings he helped Cobsworth dig and clean and then for an hour each afternoon when the sun was straight overhead and warming the canyon floor they'd open *Littell's Living Age* and work on Chad's reading lessons. In the evenings, before the light abandoned them completely, they'd practice vocabulary. Afterwards, the stars spread out across the cold sky like icing on a Sunday Social party cake, they'd talk about things. Chad came to understand Cobsworth in a way he hadn't thought he ever would. He learned about his family back east, about his winnings and losings, about a lady who captured his heart and then turned to another man.

In a lot of ways, he and Cobsworth were alike. Strange as that seemed to him, it made him think that once you got to know another person — once the barriers came down, most men had the same fears, same hopes, same challenges.

Then in the quiet moments Chad's thinking would return to McSween and Libby and the Rocking S, and he'd feel a pang at shirking his responsibilities. Winter was in the air and the shortening days brought more cold down from the north. It seemed to be coming earlier this year. Already snow capped the high peaks to the west. He ought to be persuading McSween to give him men to round up the cattle and drive them down to winter pasture, not camping out with Cobsworth learning reading, for Pete's sakes.

Probably wouldn't do any good anyway. McSween was determined to finish the dam. It seemed an obsession.

It was the evening of the third day after lessons and easy conversations were over when, with a blanket over his shoulders and the campfire warming him, he went searching for the small pouch of tobacco and papers. He discovered the wrinkled telegram in his vest pocket. Pressing it smooth in the light of the fire, he attempted to put to practical use some of what Cobsworth had tried to teach him. But the words scribbled on it didn't look anything at all like what he'd been taught.

His lessons had been from neatly printed pages, easy to cipher what each letter was and then employ the sound of that letter to work out the word. That was the hard part. Once he managed to get the letters into a sound, he knew what the word meant — most of the time. But the telegram was different. The message was not printed in neat letters but scrawled in bold, flowing hand-written letters that might as well have been Latin, another language Cobsworth knew passably well. He frowned. In order to really know how to read, he was going to have to learn the trick twice!

"Something I can help you with?" Cobsworth, having seen his dilemma, nodded at the telegram.

"I was counting on knowing some of the

words. Didn't figure them being different from them what's written in a book." He handed the paper across to Cobsworth.

"The words are all the same, however, when written in script the letters are formed a little differently, and they're all attached to one another like a train. Let's see what you've got here." His eyes turned down to the telegraph. He gasped. "Where did you get this?"

Cobsworth's reaction startled Chad. "One of our men dropped it."

"His name! What's his name?"

Chad was instantly alert, though he didn't know why he ought to be. "Stovill."

Cobsworth thought a moment. "I don't know that name. No matter. He has lots of men working for him."

"He? Who? Dang it, man, what does the words say?"

Cobsworth cleared his throat and peered back at the telegram. His voice sounded strained as he read it aloud:

COBSWORTH TO BE DETAINED AT ALL COSTS. THE FILLING OF THE DAM MUST BE DELAYED. SUGGEST YOU USE YOUR IMAGINATION. WILL BE ARRIVING CAÑON CITY WITHIN THE WEEK.

BRING EVIDENCE FOR EVALUA-
TION.

OCM

Chad whistled. "Stovill's a hired gun."

"He must have been the man who tried to shoot me."

"That was the morning Stovill went into Cañon City to fetch back some dynamite." His eyes narrowed. "But he wasn't alone." Chad sorted through his thoughts as he spoke. "Terry Filbert was along with him. I knew Filbert a lot of years. He'd never have allowed it."

"Knew?"

"Filbert was killed four days ago — same day you were bushwhacked. There was an explosion."

"What kind of explosion?"

"That dynamite they brought back." Chad thought it over, the bits and pieces coming together like a puzzle. He should have seen it. How was he so blind? He looked at Cobsworth and couldn't be sure if it was fear or just confusion he saw in his face. "Who is OCM? Do the initials mean anything to you?"

"Absolutely! I thought you knew. His name appears in newspapers all the time these days. They stand for Othniel Charles

Marsh."

"Marsh?" The name was familiar, then he remembered. "The bone-hunter fellow you told me about a while back."

"The very one, and now he wants to steal my discovery! He wants to take credit for finding it. He wants *my* dinosaur! Well, he isn't going to get it!" Cobsworth reached for his little rifle.

"Calm down, Cobsworth. This Marsh fellow hasn't got his fingers on your bones yet. You figured it was him behind it, that day you was bushwhacked. You started to say so, then stopped."

"How could he have learned of it? The only other person who knew was Ralph, the student assistant who helped me during the summer." He eyes stretched. "You don't suppose he told Marsh, do you?"

"You trust him?"

"Ralph is a loyal chap. He wouldn't betray me."

"There are ways to make a man talk. Some not too pleasant. The Injuns know a lot of 'em."

"My God, you don't suppose —" Cobsworth's Adam's apple bobbed. "What are we going to do?"

We? Chad wouldn't be dragged into this except for Stovill. Stovill had lied to Mc-

Sween and it appeared he had something to do with Filbert's death. That made it personal. Cobsworth wasn't dragging him into anything he wasn't already involved in. The more he thought about it, his anger burned toward Stovill. "I'll tend to Stovill in the morning. Far as this Marsh fellow goes, we still have a couple days."

"Maybe not. The telegram said within a week. He might be here anytime." Cobsworth's voice squeaked. "He might already be here."

"I'll head out first light. After I deal with Stovill, I'll see about this Marsh fellow."

"What if they come for my dinosaur tonight?"

"I don't expect they will, but you never can tell." Chad took the Sharps from the rifle scabbard, checked the load in the chamber and laid it near his bedroll.

Cobsworth paced, moving in and out of the firelight. It made Chad nervous.

"You'll wear a hole in the ground."

"Sorry." He hunkered by the fire, fidgeting there on his haunches.

"Try to get some sleep." It was getting colder and Chad crawled under his blanket while Cobsworth warmed his hands at the fire mumbling something about it being *his* dinosawer!

And that was the last Chad recalled before drifting off to sleep.

CHAPTER 16

Chad startled awake. The sky was gray, the air cold. He strained in the silence for whatever it was that had alerted him. He heard nothing at first except a chill wind buffeting the canyon wall and the faint murmur of water trickling down the steep floor. Mixed in with these, a quiet tapping sound of someone or something just beyond the shadowy shoulder of rock.

He eased his fingers around the revolver under the blanket. The night had brought a heavy frost and the stiff blanket crackled beneath a coat of brittle ice crystals.

The tapping stopped. Chad held his breath, listening. It started up again — a sharp noise like . . . like bone striking rock. Then he exhaled a gray puff of steam and a small grin moved across his face. *A mite on the nervous side this morning, aren't you, Chad?*

He hitched himself up on one elbow.

Twenty yards off an antlered buck raised its heavy head from the stream and looked back at Chad. Three does froze in place like statues, their wide eyes riveted. All at once, like explosions on four legs, the animals wheeled about and fled out of the canyon, their slim black hooves clattering upon the rocky floor.

"What!" Cobsworth shrieked, throwing off his blanket and leaping to his feet. He hopped up and down dressed only in his long handles and stocking feet. "What was that?"

"Just some deer out for breakfast."

He shifted his feet on the cold ground. "Oh. Is that all? They startled me." He stood there a moment staring into the darkness then lifted a foot and peered at it. "What is this? Frost?"

"That time of year, Cobsworth." Chad threw off his blanket and pulled on his boots. "Whoa!" He stomped his feet to get the blood circulating, pulled on a jacket and wandered into the trees, returning a few minutes later feeling relieved. They kindled the cook fire and hunkered near the flames. Cobsworth warmed his hands while the water in the coffeepot began to boil.

"You're going after him today, Chad?"

Chad nodded. "Only hope he didn't cause

more mischief while I was away. Should have showed you that telegram soon as I arrived but I forgot all about it."

"Well, you can't blame yourself for that." Cobsworth poured the coffee and the hot tin cups felt good in the cold air.

They drank without talking, each man filled with his own thoughts. Chad tapped his cup on a rock, knocking out the grounds at the bottom and stood. "Keep your eyes peeled while I'm away. Can you hit anything with that pip-squeak rifle you have there?"

"It's a Stevens," he replied as if that answered the question.

"But can you hit anything?"

"I'm a fair shot," he retorted, sounding irritated that Chad should question his marksmanship.

"Good. Keep your Stevens handy till I get back. Just don't shoot it unless you have to. Wounded men shoot back, and a twenty-two most likely will make 'em more mad than hurt. Another thing. Don't do any more bone digging."

Chad went to his horse and hefted the saddle onto its back.

"Stop working? Why?"

Chad pulled the cinch tight and shoved a boot in the stirrup. The worn seat felt comfortable, a place where he belonged.

"When you're working on them bones your brain gets derailed. Stovill could march a whole army up behind you and you'd not hear them."

Cobsworth frowned, his eyes showing hurt, but he knew what Chad had said was true. "I suppose you're right. I'll try to be more aware of my surroundings."

"I'll be back in a couple days." Chad clucked his horse ahead then stopped and looked back at Cobsworth standing there, his gangly arms making the jacket he wore look too short. "Take care of yourself." It was different this time. Cobsworth had stopped being an annoyance and had become a friend. Chad was more than a little worried about the bone digger as he rode out of the canyon.

Corky Rye stuck his head out of the back of the chuck wagon and gave Chad a lopsided smile as he rode into camp. "Started to worry about you, Chad. Was about to call a search party. Vittles run out?" Corky crawled out of the wagon dragging a heavy Dutch oven after him.

Chad leaned forward in his saddle and gazed at the dam. Rocking S wranglers were busy upon it like ants on a hill. Already new scaffolding had sprouted atop it looking like a skeleton of bones. He grinned to himself. Would he have thought of it that way before meeting Cobsworth? His face turned grim, remembering what he was there to do. "Where's Stovill?"

Corky set the big iron pot on the ground and wiped his shirtsleeve across his brow. "A day late and a dollar short. Alex pulled out day before yesterday. Said his back hurt and he was going to find hisself real work suitable for a cowboy. Truth to be told, Chad, he never struck me as much of a wrangler to begin with, the way he coddled that rifle of his and shunned the animals. I figured him for a dude. Anyway, he rode back to the outfit to collect his due. My guess he's long gone from these parts by now."

Stovill might have quit the ranch, but he'd not gone far. Cañon City was but half a day's ride. That's where Chad figured he'd find him. But first he needed to make one more stab at getting those cows down from the high country. McSween should have sense enough to see the time was short. Chad headed back to headquarters.

Riders appeared on the horizon from the direction of the ranch house. Three, maybe four. Chad rode to the crest of a hill for a better look. The riders came nearer, three of 'em, coming at a gallop, McSween in the lead. Libby was with him, and another man. Bristol, Chad determined a minute or two later.

He got his horse moving and met up with them. McSween drew rein, a dangerous scowl darkening his face. Libby wasn't smiling either, her hard eyes cutting lines deep into her cheeks, driving out the natural beauty of her face. He guessed the cause of her anger. Of late keeping a man on her leash was becoming something of a challenge for her. It was the storm brewing behind McSween's fierce blue eyes that brought the hairs on the nape of Chad's neck ramrod straight. But it was Libby who spoke first.

"You're willfully going against Father's wishes," she snarled, anger flaring her nostrils. "We all know what you've been doing, where you've been."

"Be quiet, Libby Ellen!" McSween barked, narrowing his icy eyes at Chad. "What's this nonsense I hear about you packing in a month's supply of grub for that bone digger?"

"Don't deny it! Alex told us what you've done." Libby put on a sly smile.

Suddenly Chad knew the game Stovill was playing. If he couldn't scare Cobsworth out

of Thunder Canyon, he'd twine the Mc-
Sweens around his finger like a string pup-
pet and make them throw him out.

"Elizabeth Ellen! Not another outburst!"

Chad said, "Where's Stovill now?"

"Are the allegations true?" McSween said
in a low voice.

"I took him some grub."

"Dammit, Chad, you knew my feelings
toward that bone digger. Aiding and abet-
ting —"

"Stop the schoolmarm talk, C. L.! This
isn't a court of law and you're no judge."

"Chadwick!"

He ignored her. "The trouble is, you don't
know the half of what's been going on here.
You've been blinded by that dam of yours
and it's about to ruin you. You ain't got two
good wranglers left riding watch on your
cattle. They're all down in Thunder Canyon
sweating like gandydancers for Harrison
while half your herd is still up on high
pastures with snow coming early this year."

"Are you quite finished?"

"I ain't hardly begun, C. L., but I ain't
got the time to go into it with you here. I'm
asking again. Where's Stovill?"

Libby flinched and turned her face from
him.

McSween said, "What has Stovill got to

180

do with any of this?"

"I don't know the facts yet, but I'm pretty sure he's responsible for the explosion, for the death of those men, and for bushwhacking Cobsworth."

"No!" Libby said.

The fire in McSween's eyes dampened some. "You have any proof, Chad?"

"I found this on Stovill." Chad handed him the wrinkled telegram. "Soon as I find him, I'll get whatever proof we need."

McSween glanced at the telegram and his face went slack and he seem unable to think of a reply. He passed it to Bristol. Bristol read it and said, "Stovill drew his pay and rode off yesterday."

"Did he say where?"

"He mentioned Cañon City."

"That's where I figured he'd head to."

Libby snatched the telegram from Bristol. She gave a startled gasp, her eyes widening as she read.

Bristol said, "If it's true, Chad. He needs to be brought in."

"I know." Chad reined his horse around and started toward Cañon City.

CHAPTER 17

Chad rode down the middle of Macon Street, a fall wind gusting between the brick buildings, curling a snaky trail of dust across the street ahead of him. The townspeople who were out and about strolled along the sidewalk from shop to shop, women with a hand held upon their bonnets, men holding onto the brim of their Stetsons or bowlers.

In the valley of the Arkansas River, apple orchards were beginning to appear in abundance, a sure sign that civilization had arrived. Another sign was the gray walls of the new State Prison, partly hidden behind a procession of dark walnut trees. It had originally been intended as a Territorial Prison when first begun in 1870. Statehood changed all that a few years later. During the summer months the prison grew its own vegetables. Today, brown vines lie withered upon the rich dark earth, victims of an early frost. The valley of the Arkansas, having first been settled by the Ute Indians seeking a mild-weather retreat from the harsh cold of the surrounding mountains, had become a refuge for Eastern sodbusters.

Chad frowned. Like the mountain men and the beaver, the Injuns were mostly gone. The first white men moved into the area in 1859 bringing their tools, laws, guns. They built crude wooden houses and called the place Town of Canyon City, only some reporter used the Spanish spelling Cañon City and that's how it went down on record in 1861.

Now, spanking brand-new brick buildings sprouted like bright flowers between the fading remains of the old gray wooden beginnings of Cañon City. The brick kilns in nearby Florence were doing a booming business.

The shadow that had followed him on his left side had subtly drifted over to his right. Near one o'clock. A saloon to his left was open for business, but mostly deserted at this early hour. If there was one thing Cañon City could brag on, it was that her people were of the hardworking, God-fearing, temperate variety. The Cañon City jailhouse spent most of the time with empty cells, he mused as he reined to a halt in front of the sheriff's office.

Thinking it over, he changed his mind. This was something he wanted to handle himself. Further up the street stood Doc Bleaker's neat frame house with a picket fence and an inviting porch. Chad turned his horse toward the hitching rail out front, then took the porch steps two at a stride.

Katie Bleaker opened the door at his knock and there was a hint of surprise in her bright gray eyes. "Mr. Larimer. Come to check in on your man?"

Katie was a pretty woman who'd fared well against the years. Her long gray hair was wound up in a bun and pinned to the back of her head — a head that reached barely to Chad's shoulders. In all the years he'd known Katie, he recalled only once seeing her with her hair down and flowing free across her back, but that had been in the early hours of the morning with his chest on fire and his brain half delirious from a bullet lodged two inches from his heart. That had been a long time ago.

"How is Berryman?"

Katie frowned. "Holding his own so far. Come in. Take a seat in the parlor while I fetch Charles for you."

Chad lowered himself in a chair as Katie Bleaker disappeared down a hallway. The parlor was a pretty little room with a simple feminine elegance that only a woman's touch could lend, unlike the dark, rich masculinity of McSween's office, or the shambled furnishing of his own little cottage. Across from him was a small round table flanked by two matching cane-back chairs. A nickel-plated stove stood in the corner and showed signs of a recent cleaning and polishing. It reminded him of the cold weather coming . . .

"Hello, Chad." Doc Bleaker appeared in the hallway wearing a white shirt with its sleeves rolled and a dark vest with a watch fob dangling from one of the pockets.

"Doc." Chad stood and took Bleaker's hand. "I had some business in town and figured I'd check up on Berryman whilst I was here."

Bleaker frowned and pulled one of the cane-back chairs around, motioning Chad to sit back down.

Chad saw it in Bleaker's face. "It's looking bad, isn't it?"

"I never was much good at hiding my feelings, Chad. Truth is, it doesn't look promising. He drifts in and out of consciousness, but never fully awake. I'm trying to keep him stable, but sometimes his heart starts to race and then his breathing slows. There's not much written about the brain, although it seems every year more and more is being published in the medical journals. Still, there is so much we don't know." He spread his hands in a helpless gesture. "All we can do is wait and watch and pray. That was a costly accident, and I'm not referring to the money Mr. McSween lost."

"It wasn't an accident, Doc."

Bleaker's eyebrows lifted. "What do you mean?"

"I think the dam was deliberately blown up."

"That would make it murder."

Chad nodded.

"Who? And more importantly, why?"

"I've a pretty good idea."

Bleaker straightened in his chair, sudden interest on his face. "This is the business you spoke of?"

"It is. Have you seen any strangers hanging around town the last couple days, Doc?"

Bleaker nodded. "As a matter of fact — yesterday morning. At the depot. I was picking up a package of medical supplies when four well-dressed gentlemen got off the train. I'd never seen them before, and they appeared — how do I say it? Somehow, uncertain? Out of place?"

"Are they staying at the hotel?"

"Perhaps. I heard one of them ask the

telegrapher for direction to the livery . . . he might have inquired about the hotel, but I really wasn't paying much attention to them. By the time I retrieved my package, they had gone."

Chad thought it over. It was likely these were the men Stovill was to meet. Or they were planning to meet him somewhere.

"Do you think they're the ones you're looking for?"

"Could be. Reckon I'll just have to find them and ask."

"You should inform the constable."

Chad stood. "Do the best you can for Berryman, Doc."

"You're going after them alone?"

"It's sort of a personal matter."

"Berryman, the others . . . I can understand that, Chad. But is it smart?"

"Smart? I don't know." He went to the door.

Bleaker followed him out. "Take care of yourself."

Chad settled his hat onto his head and smiled. "Been doing that for a lot of years, Doc. Thanks."

The livery was the last building out of town before the road left Cañon City and stretched out past the gray walls of the State

Prison. Fillister Morgan raised a hand over his eyes squinting through his spectacles at the sound of Chad's footsteps. "Who's that?"

Chad moved out of the glare of the wide livery doors. Fillister lowered his hand back to the broom handle. "Oh, thought that was you, Chad."

The big barn was all in shadows, but that wasn't Morgan's problem. Everyone knew the old man was near blind and getting worse. "It's the sunlight, Fillister. You need to spend more time in the daylight."

"You got that right. I live my day in the cave. My peepers, they don't take kindly to bright no more. How you been? McSween keeping you busy? Ain't seen you in a fair piece o' time."

"I manage to fit about twenty-five hours of work into a day, Fillister."

Morgan chuckled. "What you be needing? A place fer your horse?"

"Not today. What I'm looking for is some information."

Morgan scratched the top of his balding head. "You coming to me fer infermation? Don't know as I have any to give, but fire away an' see what you hit."

"Yesterday four men arrived by train. I heard they asked about the livery."

"I remember them. City people. Suits an' ties and talking funny like they was from back east. They was looking fer a carriage to hire. I let them have an old spring wagon and Elmer."

"Elmer?" Chad cocked his head.

Morgan shrugged. "Jest a tired plug I keep around cause he reminds me of me. He's old but not quite ready to be put out to pasture yet. Elmer can still pull so long as them city gents ain't in no hurry. They didn't seem none too particular being as they paid me two dollars fer the rig and seemed pleased with what I give them."

"Did they say where they were going?"

"Nope, least not in so many words. But one of them, kinda heavy with a barbered beard, he asked about the whereabouts of Fremont Wells. I told him there was some artesian wells back in Red Canyon what some folks call Fremont Wells because John Fremont was the first white man to spy them. That's probably where you'll find them, Chad."

"It's a place to start looking. Thanks."

Morgan shifted his weight and punched his tongue into his cheek. "Why you looking for them, Chad? If it ain't none of my business, jest say so."

Chad thought it over and felt a grin move

189

across his face. "Let's just say I got a bone to pick with 'em."

CHAPTER 18

Darkness had overtaken Chad by the time
he rode into the mouth of Red Canyon, following a trail that snaked along the dry belly
of the canyon up into the mountains. Chad
let his horse pick its own way up the canyon
under the thin, cold moonlight that painted
the sandstone cliffs a ghostly pale. His eyes
darted like jackrabbits across the shadowy
landscape, pulling what details he could
from the colorless light, his ears hunting for
the faintest of sounds.

The smell of a campfire alerted him long
before the far-off flicker of yellow flames
down in a ravine became visible. Chad left
his horse tied off the trail and slipped the
rifle from its scabbard. The rise of land
separating him from the fire was choked
with scrub oak and he moved carefully
among the brittle branches, dropping noiselessly to the ground at the top.

A spring wagon sat back in the shadows

where the light of the flames could barely reach. Off a little way was the horse, tugging at the tufts of grass growing in patches near the springs. Chad spied two men near the fire and what looked like sage grouses skewered upon a spit suspended between two forked upright branches. The odor of cooking meat reminded him he'd not eaten all that day. The cold air reminded him winter was nearing. Neither of those thoughts filled him with any pleasure.

One of the men reached out from the shadows and gave the birds a turn, then he filled a glass from a bottle and sat back against a rock. Movement pulled Chad's eyes away from the fire as a stocky man strolled out of the dark and stood in the light. He squatted by the fire and inhaled deeply. "Reminds me of my boyhood, hunting in the fields with my father. You ever do any bird hunting before today, Carroway?"

The man leaning against the rock gave a short laugh and Chad detected a bitter edge in it. "Well, Professor Marsh, there weren't very many birds where I come from, and I never knew my old man. When I went hunting it was for gutter snipes or drunks and if I was in a sporting mood we'd pop off a constable or two for the hell of it."

Marsh said nothing. He stood, pulled

thoughtfully at his beard then moved out of the firelight. The third man there said, "This is a splendid location. Just before the sun went down I had an opportunity to scout along the cliffs. Judging from the strata, I'd say the rock very likely contains an abundance of fossils. It's a shame we can't take advantage of all the opportunities that present themselves."

Marsh said, "You may yet have a chance to poke around, Ganby. First we'll see what Mr. Stovill has turned up."

Ganby said, "Speaking of whom, shouldn't he have been here by now?"

Marsh grunted. "Something's delayed him. He'll be here. Mr. Stovill has a way of showing up . . . eventually."

Chad agreed with that, thinking back to when he and Eric had first met the man. Stovill did have a way of showing up.

A coyote yelped nearby and Carroway lurched to his feet. A revolver appeared in his hand, firelight catching its nickel plating and giving off bright glints as Carroway swung the weapon side to side. "What's that?"

"I believe that was a Canis Latrans," Ganby said with an indifference that bordered on contempt.

"A what?"

"A coyote, Mr. Carroway," Marsh said. "Put that thing away."

"Oh." Carroway slipped the revolver back into the shoulder holster beneath his jacket and glared at the other man. "Next time talk English, Ganby."

"Sorry, Carroway. I keep forgetting —"

Marsh put a warning hand upon Ganby's shoulder. Ganby took the warning and said no more.

Carroway let the incident drop and turned back to their food. "Looks to me like these birds are fit to eat, Prefessor." Carroway lifted the spit and pushed the birds off it with the blade of a knife, then cut them apart.

The men gathered around the fire preparing to eat their dinner while Chad lay in the dark, cold and hungry, not thirty feet from them.

"Either of you two seen Taft?" Marsh asked, settling into a folding chair.

Carroway said, "He went off some time ago. Probably had to take a leak. I don't expect he's got his nose buried in a pile of bones, but you never know." He laughed. "You fellows are a strange lot." It was clear Carroway held Marsh's occupation in the same low regard as apparently Marsh and Ganby held Carroway's. Chad figured theirs was a partnership of necessity. Marsh needed protection and Carroway needed the money Marsh paid for it.

"Want me to go look for him?" Ganby asked.

Marsh grunted. "No. I don't want to have to go looking for you too. He'll come back when his stomach tells him it's time."

Taft would be the fourth man that Doc Bleaker had seen getting off the train. They were all here. It wasn't but a few minutes later that Chad heard footsteps crashing through the underbrush and passing in the dark near him.

Marsh looked over his shoulder. "Where'd you get off to, Taft?"

"A little stroll to get the blood circulating. Darn cold tonight. Dinner ready?"

"We've started without you."

Taft pulled around a three-legged stool and the four of them ate and drank and spent the evening huddled in woolen blankets, feeding juniper branches into the fire.

Chad had no blanket and was half tempted to go down and join them since they wouldn't know who he was or his connection to Stovill. But he didn't. He'd been cold before, and when Stovill did show up, Chad wanted to keep the advantage of surprise.

An hour passed. They spoke of things Chad didn't understand and from time to time wondered what was delaying Stovill. Chad wanted to know too. After a while they curled up in their blankets and let the fire die down. Chad sat in the shadows waiting, rubbing warmth into his arms, listening to the quiet night sounds, remembering the odor of cooking meat, growing drowsy.

It was long past midnight when the gentle footfalls of approaching horses snapped him awake. He shivered as he peered hard into the darkness. The fire below had burned down to a few red embers around which the four men slept. The spring wagon stood out stark and cold in the pale moonlight. The horse down there heard them coming. His head lifted suddenly and his ears twitched forward.

Warmth surged through Chad as his heart quickened. His hand flexed stiffly around the rifle across his legs, the tingling leaving his fingers, his grip firming.

Three animals emerged from the shadows and halted near the men who slept on, their city-dulled senses making them vulnerable. A man who spent many a night sleeping out under an open sky soon learned to sleep with one ear alert. If he didn't, he was liable to continue sleeping for all eternity.

Alexander Stovill, riding the lead horse, peered down at them and a pleased grin flashed across his lips. Riding in without them knowing it was just a game to him, and as usual, he held the winning hand.

Chad's view shifted to the second rider. Cobsworth! His thoughts took on a worried edge. Cobsworth's hands were tied behind his back and he seemed to be having trouble keeping himself straight in the saddle. Stovill held the reins to Cobsworth's horse and to his mule, which had a bundle tied to its back.

Stovill dropped quietly to the ground and with the toe of his boot nudged Carroway.

The gunman came awake, looked around, then grinned and levered himself up on one elbow. "Al. What happened? You was supposed to be here hours ago."

"Had to take a back way. Had riders on my tail."

Carroway came suddenly alert. "Were you followed here?"

Stovill gave a quiet laugh. "Left them crisscrossing their own trails back up in the mountains. I swung wide and worked down from the high country. Don't worry. It'll take more savvy than McSween has to follow the trail I laid down."

Carroway grinned. "If he does, it'll be the

last trail he'll ever follow, heh, Al?"

Stovill nodded at the revolver that had appeared in Carroway's hand. "You'd like to pop off someone this trip, wouldn't you, Kenny?"

"Gotta keep up my practice."

Stovill hooked a thumb over his shoulder at Cobsworth. "Maybe you can pop off that one. Excess baggage once Marsh gets done with him, far as I can see. Don't want to leave anyone behind who can point a finger at us."

Carroway glanced over and made a face. "I prefer them moving a little, Al."

Stovill laughed and Marsh came awake at the sound. "Stovill?" He rubbed the sleep from his eyes.

"Expecting Professor Cope instead?" He bent over the fire ring and sprinkled twigs onto the coals, blowing a small flame to life.

Marsh threw off his blanket and stood. "Problems?"

The flames grew and flickered orange light over the two men's faces.

"Nothing I couldn't take care of."

"Let me be the judge of that."

Stovill's head jerked up, his eyes narrowing. "It's what you pay me to do."

"I expect things to go smoothly, with no

problems, Alexander. *That's* what I pay you to do."

For a moment the two men locked eyes, then Stovill smiled. "I told you I took care of it. Just a bunch of hicks and a mixed-up girl with stars in her eyes. They were, however, very pretty eyes. I left them riding in circles back in those mountains." He hitched his chin to the west. "Laid down a trail even an Indian couldn't follow."

Chad figured there were mighty few trails McSween couldn't cipher, given enough time, but Stovill was brimming over with confidence just the same.

"I certainly hope so . . ." Marsh's words trailed off as he saw Cobsworth. "Why did you bring him?" he growled, startling Taft and Ganby awake.

"Couldn't very well leave him. He knew me right off, knew I worked for you. You want a *smooth* operation, right?"

"Damn."

"It's a problem easily remedied. Isn't that right, Kenny?"

Carroway chuckled.

"I didn't want anyone hurt."

"A little late for that, Professor."

"What do you mean?"

"You wanted the dam delayed. That didn't come cheap. Your *smooth* operation has

199

already cost the lives of three men. What does one more matter?"

"This is awful," Marsh stammered. "Men killed. And that one over there, one of Cope's associates."

"Another reason he can't be left behind."

"It wasn't supposed to be like this, Alexander!"

"You'd rather the board of directors at that museum of yours find out how you have acquired such a fine collection of bones? Your reputation isn't exactly pristine as it is, Professor. The newspapers would love to get a hold of this story. Cope would love it too."

"Cope isn't pristine, either," Marsh shot back.

"All the more reason he'd want you discredited."

In the uncertain light Marsh's eyes were dark shadows but Chad sensed the torment in them. When he finally spoke, his words were low, weighed down with heavy emotion. "Unfortunately, Alexander, I see no other way, either."

"It's the only way." Stovill went to the horses and hauled Cobsworth to the ground, taking him to the spring wagon and tying him to the spokes of a wheel. He returned to the animals and began working at the knots that held the bundle to Cobsworth's mule. "Someone give me a hand here."

Marsh motioned to Ganby. Together they carried the bundle to the fire and set it on the ground. Stovill stepped back. "Proof you asked for, proof you have. Go on, Professor, open it up."

Marsh studied him a moment then knelt and began tugging at the ropes. The canvas fell away.

"Proof enough, Professor?" Stovill asked.

Marsh had already snatched a ruler from his coat pocket and was busily laying it at different directions across the skull.

Stovill laughed softly. "Kenny, is that wine any good?"

Carroway fetched the bottle and shook it near his ear. "Must have been. Ain't nary a swallow left. Got another bottle in the wagon."

Chad had seen all he needed to. Pushing back from the ridge, he move quietly down the back side and through the brush. Making a wide swing, he came to the edge of a clearing and hunkered there, studying the spring wagon from the other side. Between it and himself were the horses and mule, and since animals get fidgety when someone comes up on them unexpected, all he could do for now was wait.

CHAPTER 19

The waiting stretched out while Marsh and Ganby studied the big skull Stovill had delivered to them. From his vantage point, Chad saw that Cobsworth had stopped struggling at the ropes, still now with his chin down on his chest. Finally, Taft wandered over to the animals and pulled off their saddles and the pack frame. He hauled the tack near the wagon then led the stock off to where Elmer was tethered near the water. Across the way, Stovill and Carroway were sharing a bottle of wine and a story about a woman they both knew. For the moment, they were all occupied.

Chad moved out in a crouch and dropped quietly into the shadow behind the wagon. On the far side a pair of tied hands poked through the wheel spokes. Cobsworth's head jerked off his chest as though trying to fight off sleep. A moment later Taft strode back into camp and dragged his stool closer to the other two bone diggers.

"What do you think, Professor Marsh? Is it the genuine article?"

"Yes indeed, Mr. Taft! I must have the rest of specimen. We shall proceed to Thunder Canyon first thing tomorrow."

Stovill glanced up. "That's taking a risk, Professor."

"It can't be helped, Alexander. This is far too important a discovery to allow it to disappear beneath the water."

Cobsworth straightened up at that, glaring across at them. Chad had to keep him from speaking. He fingered a pebble and tossed it at Cobsworth's shoe, but Cobsworth didn't seem to notice. Chad tossed another that bounced off his shoulder. Cobsworth went stiff.

"Cobsworth," Chad whispered.

The bone digger leaned back against the wheel. "Chad? Is that you?" He had enough sense to keep his voice low.

"Don't look around. I'm going to cut the ropes. Keep your hands in back like they're still tied."

Cobsworth nodded.

Chad sliced the cords, and Cobsworth rubbed his wrists. "When did you get here?"

"Never mind that. We need to get you out

of here before they know what's happening."

"It was Stovill, Chad. You were right. It was he who shot at me. All the way here he bragged on how he'd won over your confidence, and McSween's, and that girl, McSween's daughter."

A pang squeezed his chest hearing that, realizing how easily she'd fallen for his lies, how easily they had all been taken in by the flimflammer. "He did that for sure."

"He got a jump on me before I could reach my rifle."

"That's just as well. He'd have killed you if you had."

Cobsworth's shoulders gave a small heave. "You're right. In spite of what I said back there, I'm not really much of a rifleman."

"That don't matter."

"As we were heading up the canyon McSween showed up with some riders. Stovill managed to keep them pinned down. His rifle seemed to have a much greater range than their weapons. After a while Stovill managed to lose them."

Stovill's laugh from the fire cut off Cobsworth's words just then. The gunman was tipping up the wine bottle and shaking it out. "Looks like we run up against a dry hole here, Kenny."

"Never fear, old friend." Carroway's voice slurred and he reached around to a canvas sack and produced a fresh bottle.

Chad said softly, "No slicker like Stovill will run McSween onto a cold trail for very long. Many a brash Injun has tried and they all bellied up in the end. McSween ain't nobody's fool."

"If those two keep drinking like that, in another hour we'll be able to walk out of here without them ever knowing we're gone."

"There's not an hour left in this night. It'll be dawning soon." He studied the terrain from this new angle. "I'm going to circle around to the far side of that ridge. When I get there I'll fire a shot. That will turn their heads, maybe even pull the hired guns out of camp to see what's going on. When they ain't looking, get clear of here and find someplace to hole up."

"And yourself?"

"I'll be moving. Don't worry about me. Take care of your own skin. Put distance between you and Stovill's gun then go to ground and stay put. Got it?"

"Yes. I've got it."

"I'm moving out now. Get ready to do the same."

"Be careful."

Chad eased back and the shadows were waiting to take him. He swung wider this time, keeping to the dark, skirting open ground. Finding the scrub oak again, he moved quiet as a wisp of smoke until he reached the ridge, looking down on the men around the fire. He glanced at the sky, faintly graying to the east. The darkness wasn't going to last long. Stovill's and Carroway's voices reached him, their language courser than it had been earlier, the wine muddling their words. So much the better for what Chad knew he had to do. He recalled that first night and how Stovill and McSween carried on about their schools. Yale! Chad scoffed to himself. He'd bet twenty dollars to a worn-down horseshoe the closest Mr. Alexander Stovill the Second ever got to that notable institution was the front gate. Bile burned the back of his throat. There was a score to settle up for sure. He backed from the ridgeline then stopped suddenly when a word from below reached his ears.

"Filbert was his name. Harrison sent him with me to help load the dynamite. I told him I didn't need help, but the colonel insisted. Having Filbert along was the last thing I needed with what I had to do."

"So what did you do?" Carroway asked.

"What could I do? I had to get rid of him somehow. We drove into town and I said I had an errand to run and left him loading the stuff while I went to the telegraph office to get the professor's telegram. I got back, helped him finish up, and a couple miles out of town said I had to piss. Went round back of the buckboard and put a bullet between his shoulders. Hid the body under the tarp and drove over to the canyon where Cobsworth was working and found a place on the rim where I had a clear shot and commenced to making him dance. But Larimer showed up so I made a quick exit." Stovill laughed. "Should have seen it, Kenny, Cobsworth had his arms over his head hopping like a kangaroo. He hid behind a rock but I still had a clean shot."

"Why didn't you take it?"

"The professor's telegram said not to hurt him." Stovill shrugged. "I should have plugged him when I had the chance and let the professor stew on it. Turns out we're going have to kill him anyway."

Carroway nodded. "You ought to know by now, never go against your better judgment, Alex. What about the fellow you shot? How'd you explain that?"

"Arranged for a dynamite accident. Got rid of the body and stopped the building of the dam all at the same time." He gave a short laugh. "But I got a little careless and nearly blew my own head off. Oh well, it all worked out. Now pass that bottle over here."

Carroway sounded like he'd drunk too much, while Stovill still seemed to have a clear head. He'd be the more dangerous of the two. From where he watched, Chad had a clear shot, but the notion of back-shooting a man churned irritably in his gut. Added to that, the range was on the long side for a revolver and the Sharps was a single shot. It would be risky trying to take them both out now, and he'd learned from the mountaineers of his youth that when you're up against a pack of Injuns, your odds lay in singling them out one by one. It was always better to make them come to the medicine.

He backed away, drew his revolver and fired it in the air then dodged to the west where the scrub oak was thicker. It didn't take but a moment before Stovill and Carroway showed their silhouettes on the ridge. Chad held his place, giving Cobsworth time to skeddadle to safety.

The two gunman split up, Stovill going east and Carroway coming straight toward Chad. He found himself frowning and none too happy at what he knew he had to do next.

Then a branch snapped. Chad drew in a breath, his hand tightening about the grips of the revolver as someone moved nearby. He braced himself, his heart hammering, but at the last minute he drew back. It was the bone digger, Ganby. The man crashed past him in the dark. Chad waited until he'd gone by then stepped out and brought the revolver down hard. Ganby crashed to the ground.

Ganby hadn't gone down quietly. Chad sprinted a dozen steps up the slope, still among the heavier growth.

"Ganby . . . Ganby . . . where'd you go?" Taft whispered, moving carelessly among the branches in the dark. Chad let him pass unharmed. He'd find his unconscious friend and that would keep him busy enough. It wasn't the bone diggers Chad was worried about. It was the two Eastern gunmen, and in the dark, Chad had lost track of both of them.

A quiet rustling told him someone was moving down from the ridge to his right. Silently, Chad circled toward the sound. His boot came down on a twig with a sharp snap.

He stopped.

The darkness went strangely still, then something shiny glinted in the failing moonlight. Chad leaped to one side as the orange tongue of flame licked out at him, the bark of the shot so near it set his ears ringing. He felt the hammer blow in his leg, then he crashed through dark branches and hit the ground hard.

A second shot burst the night. Chad swung his rifle and pulled the trigger. The big Sharps boomed and in the flash he saw Carroway's arms fling wide, and then the light was gone. Chad yanked his revolver from its holster and waited. After a few moments the fire began, making itself known in quickly growing leaps until Chad's whole leg burned. He felt down his trouser leg. Blood was flowing, soaking the cloth. He tore off his bandanna and twisted it around his thigh, using a short stick to turn it tight.

There was no time to do more. The shots would bring Stovill. Chad pulled himself to his feet using a branch for support. Holding the tourniquet tight, he limped up the ridge, passing Carroway's body laying facedown. What he saw made him stop. The big fifty had taken the gunman in the chest, tearing a hole out his back big enough to put a fist through. He grimaced at the bloody sight, his heart numb. He felt nothing but the mounting pain that set his teeth hard together. Later, the memory would haunt him, but he had no time for that now.

Only Marsh remained in the campsite, pacing near the fire. Cobsworth had fled. Chad hoped the bone digger had found someplace safe to hole up. Taft would be helping Ganby nurse a frightful headache and Carroway was out of the picture permanently. That left only Stovill.

The sky had faded to purple where it touched down against the dark land and the undersides of the high clouds had taken on a rose tint. Below, the shadows were beginning to lift. Chad backed away from the ridge and halted among the trees to examine the wound. It was still bleeding in spite of the tourniquet, although the flow had slowed. He gave the stick another half turn.

"Larimer!"

Chad's head jerked around.

Stovill's voice called again from the other side of the ridge Chad had just descended. "I know you can hear me. Come out. We can talk."

Chad struggled up the slope and pushed his head up over the ridge. Stovill stood among the junipers on the far side of their campsite below. He had an arm around Cobsworth and his revolver against the bone digger's head. Marsh, staring at them from the other side of the smoldering campfire, had gone rigid, as though startled at Stovill's sudden arrival.

"I've got your friend. Come out where I can see you. I'll hold my fire."

Fear for Cobsworth squeezed at Chad's chest along with a growing awareness that his thoughts had begun to take on a dull, fuzzy edge. Distantly, he wondered how much blood he'd lost. His fist tightened on the tourniquet. He couldn't think about that now. He forced his thoughts to sharpen. "Let him go. We'll talk then."

Stovill's view shifted toward the ridge at the sound of Chad's voice. "Ah, over there." He laughed. "Not a chance, my friend. Come out where I can see you or Cobsworth gets it."

"Don't worry about me, Chad!"

Stovill rapped Cobsworth's head with the barrel of his revolver. "You better worry about him, Larimer."

"Alexander!"

"Stay out of this, Professor."

"You work for me, Alexander. You will put that gun away."

"Sorry, Professor, I just resigned. You want to stay healthy, you'll keep out of this."

Marsh's mouth screwed down tight, his fists balling with anger.

"How about it, cowboy? You going to

show yourself or does your friend become extinct, like those bones?"

Stovill had enough of the devil in him to do exactly what he threatened to do, and Chad was running out of time. He shook his head, trying to clear his muddled thoughts. Sweat beaded upon his brow, yet his skin had become cold. "Okay. I'm coming out." Chad stood, swaying.

Stovill grinned. "That's more like it. Come join the party."

Gritting back the pain, tourniquet grasped tight, Chad staggered down the tilted land.

"You're limping? Carroway's bullet?"

Chad came into camp. "Carroway's bullet."

"Dead?"

"Back there . . . somewhere."

Stovill's dark face, half hidden behind Cobsworth's shoulder, never flinched. If he felt anything over Carroway's death, he wasn't showing it. Cobsworth's face had blanched and his eyes stood wide.

"Too bad. We'd had some fun times together. I kind of thought Carroway had bought the farm when I heard that big rifle of yours go off. I didn't think it prudent to hunt around in the dark for you. Cobsworth, on the other hand, he was easy to find, crashing around like a shot elk. He was just the ticket I needed."

"Never figured you for a man who needed a ticket anywhere. You make your own way and your own rules as you go along. He's no threat to you Stovill. Let him go."

"Never considered him one, Chad, but you on the other hand . . . Once you're out of the way I might consider letting him live. But I rather doubt it. Don't like leaving a witness lying about."

"Does that include me too, Alexander? I'm a witness."

"You, Professor?" Stovill laughed. "I've got the goods on you, plenty enough to keep your tongue from wagging — you and the others." Stovill glanced around. "Speaking of Taft and Ganby, where are they?"

Chad's head had become light and for a moment Stovill drifted out of focus. Chad took a sharp breath, clearing his vision, steadying himself. "Ganby's gonna have a headache when he comes to. Taft is probably with him."

Stovill's voice lowered. "So that just leaves you and me, Larimer." There was a hard edge to his words, a finality that brought a moment of instant clarity to Chad's brain.

Chad's hand lowered to the revolver on his hip, tingling like he'd slept on it. He flexed his fingers to get the blood moving, and out the corner of his eye, Marsh backed off a step or two. There was still Cobsworth. Chad's mouth went dry. He swallowed to loosen the knot of tension tying his throat. "You're good with a gun, Stovill. No need to hide behind a man to do your shooting."

"You're right. I am good. But I watched how you took on those rustlers that morning. You got the courage, Chad, and the will to see it through, and that's a dangerous mixture. I suspect you can handle a gun with more competency than you care to let on." Stovill turned his gun on Chad.

In that instant, Cobsworth drove the heel of his work boot into Stovill's instep. Stovill yelped and Cobsworth turned out of Stovill's startled grip. Stovill spun around with murder in his eyes, but before he could fire, Cobsworth shot a short, hot jab to the man's chin and the gun fired into the air. Cobsworth followed it up with a hammering volley to Stovill's gut. The gun slipped from Stovill's hand as he tried to cover his face and his belly, and swing a wide arm in Cobsworth's direction.

Chad's brain floated, his eyes having trouble staying focused so that he wasn't sure he was seeing Cobsworth dancing back, ducking and dodging, prancing like a colt, fists wheeling like a windmill. With a mesmerizing grace, the division champion of 1863 waltzed around Stovill, punching holes in his defenses. Cobsworth's feet seemed to leave the ground. Chad shook his head to clear the fog.

Knuckles pummeled bone and skin with a sprightly cadence that sent Stovill backpedaling. No longer able to mount a defense, Stovill had all he could do to stay on his feet. Cobsworth moved in for the kill, his long arms snapping out like steam pistons. Two to Stovill's face, three quick jabs to his stomach bending him forward, then a roundhouse to his chin.

With a teeth-grinding crash, Stovill's head snapped back and that was the end of it. The gunman hit the ground with a thud and didn't move. Chad felt his own legs giving way. He tottered and went to his knees, a sword thrust of pain shooting up his leg.

CHAPTER 20

Standing over Stovill's crumpled shape, fists still poised, Cobsworth took a careful step backward and then looked worriedly at Chad. Then Cobsworth's head snapped around at the sound of fast approaching horses.

In spite of the bees swarming his ears, Chad heard them too, but his eyes were having trouble focusing. In the thin light all he could make out was a blur of movement, the creak of saddle leather and the jangle of spurs.

His head had begun to spin from the loss of blood.

"Chad!" Libby's voice reached him through the murky distance. Then her face was near his, her blue eyes large with concern. "You're hurt."

His mouth was dry and filled with cotton balls. He worked some moisture into it. "Leg."

"Got to get the bleeding stopped." Her voice was firm and her hand grasped his where it still gripped the tourniquet.

Another person came near and the sharp odor of a recently smoked cigar reached Chad's nose. Chad more sensed than saw him. "Here, let me have at it, Libby." The tourniquet bit down harder as McSween gave it a bear-paw turn.

"Chad." It was Cobsworth's voice. "You're going to be all right, Chad." The bone digger's concerned face swam into view.

Chad drew in a breath that cleared his head a little, sharpening his vision. "You stomped him on the foot, Cobsworth. Not exactly — what'd you called it? Gentlemanly fisticuffs?"

Cobsworth's mouth quirked and a smile came to his eyes. "As a friend once informed me, out west one does not always have the luxury of following the Marquis of Queensberry rules."

"Can't say as I've ever seen such fancy footwork. I am indeed impressed. Didn't think you had it in you."

"What happened here, Chad?" McSween demanded.

"Father. Not now."

Chad looked up into the great, bearded face. "Cobsworth can tell you. Or you can get it out of Marsh."

"Marsh?" McSween said.

Cobsworth said, "Professor Marsh headed up over the ridge once Stovill was down for the count. He appeared to be in a rather urgent retreat."

"Who are you? You the bone digger?"

"Err . . . yes, sir, Mr. McSween."

"Want me to go after him, boss?" That was Bristol's voice.

McSween shook his head. "We got a more urgent matter to take care of here. Let him go. He probably has his own remuda of Philadelphia lawyers that'll get him off anyway." McSween looked toward Stovill. "Better throw a rope on that one before he comes to."

A fog blurred Chad's eyes as a bone-numbing cold spread through him. Consciousness grew thin and for a while he floated in an icy haze. But he could still hear them talking.

"Look. Up there, boss," Bristol said. "Two more, and one of 'em's staggering like he's drunk."

Cobsworth said, "That's Mr. Ganby and Mr. Taft. Marsh's associates."

"Round 'em up, Bristol," McSween growled. "Looks like we have us a couple of the yahoos after all."

"Father," Libby said in an urgent voice. "We need to get Chad to Doctor Bleaker. I fear the bullet has hit an artery. He's still bleeding."

"I'll hitch a horse to that wagon." McSween's voice became thin and reedy, and that was the last Chad remembered.

From his straight-back chair, Chad stared past Katie Bleaker's delicate white curtains at the snow drifting gently to the ground. A frown tipped the corners of his mouth. Even if McSween mustered every wrangler in the territory, it would still be near impossible to get all those animals down from the high country by now. It was too late. He'd warned McSween. Told him what to expect. Somehow that didn't make Chad feel any better.

"Well?" Cobsworth asked again, raising a speculative eyebrow.

Chad turned from the window, his view moving slowly around the small room. It came to rest upon the wall by his bed. He knew that beyond it was another room the mirror image of his own, and another patient. Berryman had regained consciousness. That was something to be thankful for. Chad recalled Doc Bleaker shaking his head in quiet resignation when Chad had asked if Berryman would ever see again. Chad grimaced. It was a cross to bear. Every man had at least one.

"Well?"

Chad shifted in the chair. He never could sit still for more than five minutes without getting fidgety.

"What about those bones in Thunder Canyon?"

Cobsworth's mouth tightened to a thin, grim line. "Some things just cost too much, Chad. Those bones have commanded a high price so far. Three men's lives . . . and yours."

"Mine?" he said, surprised.

Cobsworth nodded. "You were real comfortable here before I showed up. You had friends, a place where you belonged . . . and a girl."

Chad winced. "I never really had that."

"Well, you had a life that was all together, not torn apart like it is now. Now all you have is a bullet hole in your leg and hard feelings to return to."

"It'll work out," Chad said quietly.

"You think so?"

Chad shrugged.

"So I'll ask again. What do you do now?"

"I don't know yet." He looked away as a familiar tightness pulled at his chest. Ducking and running was how he always handled the hard questions. That was how he avoided answering Cobsworth the first time he'd asked, but the question hadn't gone away.

Cobsworth drew in a breath and let it out slowly. "I'm going to return to Pennsylvania. Come with me."

"With you? You mean back east?"

"Why not?"

"Whal, I . . . I wouldn't fit in."

"Nonsense. Oh, it will take a little getting used to. Pennsylvania is nothing like Colorado, but I'll introduce you to people — some lady friends, even. You'll start to feel at home in a little while. I know a few excellent tutors who will have you reading Don Quixote in no time."

"You make it sound almost tempting. What would I do back east to earn my keep? Don't reckon there's a great need for wranglers in Pennsylvania."

"I could make you my assistant."

"Assistant?"

"I'll be applying for another grant soon and then I'll be off again to who knows where? Montana, Wyoming, or maybe even back here to Colorado. What do you say?"

Chad couldn't say anything as he tried to sort through his thoughts and feelings. That he was actually considering Cobsworth's offer surprised him. It was true, what did he have to go back to here? Considering everything, it didn't seem like a bad offer after all. "Suppose I could give it a try —"

"Chad!"

Eric's voice startled him and he turned his head. McSween, Libby and Eric stood in the doorway. Eric twisted his shoulder out of Libby's grip and ran to him.

"You ain't going to leave us, Chad, are you?" Eric's wide brown eyes were shiny.

McSween lumbered in, his bulk taking command of the small room. Libby hesitated in the doorway.

Chad said, "I didn't hear you arrive."

"Good thing," McSween said, "or I might not have overheard you conspiring to leave us. What's this foolish talk about going back east with Cobsworth?"

That was the first Chad had heard McSween refer to Cobsworth by name. Up until now it had always been "the bone digger." The two must have spent some time getting to know each other over the last few days.

"Conspiring?"

"You can't leave. You're my foreman."

"Mr. Cobsworth here is going to make me his assistant."

"A bo-bone digger? Chad, what do you

know about that?"

Chad grinned to himself. He'd never heard McSween stammer. "Once I learn my letters, I'll read up on it some." He'd already made up his mind. The sheen in Eric's eyes had confirmed his decision, but it was a rare day when someone got a rope on McSween, and he wasn't ready to let loose on it just yet.

"I got a roomful of books, Chad. No need to go off with this bone digger to learn your letters."

"Still need someone to teach me," he replied without cracking a smile.

McSween chewed his lip a moment and a slow stealthy look came to his eyes. Chad cringed a little, feeling the power of McSween's conniving mind begin to work. "All right then." His sharp blue eyes sent an icicle spear directly at Cobsworth. "I'm hiring you to stay on and teach Chad, and all my men, their letters. I'll open a schoolroom in the bunkhouse."

It was Cobsworth's turn to stammer. "Bu-but I can't do that. I have commitments back home."

McSween's mouth drew out a wide smile. "I'm afraid those commitments are going to have to wait, my friend. You see, I just came from the sheriff's office. He couldn't hold

Mr. Taft or Mr. Ganby, but he has Mr. Stovill behind bars facing murder charges, and you, Mr. Cobsworth, are a material witness for the prosecution. Since we have of recent become a state, it is within the prosecuting attorney's purview to issue a federal subpoena, should you decide to hightail it out of town."

Chad grinned. He recognized a McSween bluff when he heard one, but Cobsworth didn't. "This is awful. How . . . how long am I required to remain in Cañon City?"

McSween drew a cigar from his vest pocket and struck a match, taking a couple thoughtful puffs. "Likely the trial will happen this next spring."

Chad glanced toward the doorway, meeting Libby's eyes. She smiled briefly before looking back at her father. Well, like he'd told Cobsworth, he'd never really had her to begin with. Libby McSween Russman came with the territory. It was going to take some time to patch things up between them before they could be friends again. Lovers? Never. The thought was both tender and liberating at the same time. He didn't understand it, couldn't explain it. That was all right, though. He needed to widen his circle of friends a mite. Meeting Cobsworth had opened his eyes to that, and that was exactly what he intended to do.

"Spring!" Cobsworth stared at the big man. "Are you certain?"

McSween narrowed his view at the man. "Look at it this way. The sheriff and I are doing you a big favor. You've got something going on up in Thunder Canyon, don't you?"

"Well, ah. I'm, ah. Yes. I do, as a matter of fact." Cobsworth drew himself up to his full height and he looked McSween in the eyes. "You know that as well as I. And you disapprove of me and my work. Why the change of heart?"

"Who said anything about a change of heart!" McSween glowered, but the next instant his voice changed, quieted some, like what he had to say next was hard to get out. "I've had to pull all my men out of Thunder Canyon. They're up in the mountains riding hard to save what cows they can from starving and freezing. Lord knows, I deserve to lose every head of them." McSween glanced briefly at Chad. "I've the best foreman an outfit can have, and he warned me, but I was too obsessed to listen to him. Well, now it looks like come spring I might not have enough beef on the hoof to worry about watering, so, I'm not thinking much about the dam now, only getting my cattle down to winter pasture. And if I manage to save them, come spring I'll be too busy rounding them up and branding the young'uns to worry about building a dam. So, maybe it will be next fall before I get back to it. You understand what I'm saying, Cobsworth?"

Chad understood. McSween had been wrong and this was his way of saying it. For that big man to admit it now to Cobsworth meant he'd done some serious soul-searching these last few days.

Cobsworth nodded, his voice remarkably unemotional considering the zeal he'd previously shown about anything concerning those old bones up Thunder Canyon. "I can pursue my work for a year, with your blessing, provided I remain here as an employee."

"I pay good wages," McSween said.

"Hum." Cobsworth pursed his lips, thinking it over. "It sounds like a fair offer, Mr. McSween, but you'll have to ask my business associate before I make my decision." Cobsworth had seen and seized the advantage, and now it was his turn to tighten the thumbscrews a little.

"Business associate?"

Cobsworth sprouted a small smile and glanced at Chad.

McSween got his meaning. He cleared his throat and said, "What do you say Chad? Don't leave us. We need you . . . all of us."

Chad glanced to the doorway where Libby stiffened slightly and then walked to her father's side.

Eric gazed at him, eyes wide and hopeful.

Chad laughed and tousled the boy's sandy hair. "What do you think, pard?"

"Stay!" Eric threw his arms around him.

Chad hugged Eric. Someone had to look after the boy, to make sure he grew up with the right upbringing, with a man's influence. Besides, Chad was a cowboy not a bone digger. A good one, too. What more could a man ask out of life than that?

ABOUT THE AUTHOR

Douglas Hirt was born in Illinois. Heeding Horace Greeley's admonition to "go west, young man," he headed to New Mexico at age eighteen. Doug earned a bachelor's degree from the College of Santa Fe and a master of science degree from Eastern New Mexico University. During this time he spent several summers living in a tent in the desert near Carlsbad, New Mexico, conducting biological baseline surveys for the Department of Energy. Doug drew heavily from this "desert life" when writing his first novel, *Devil's Wind.* In 1991 Doug's novel, *A Passage of Seasons,* won the Colorado Authors' League Top Hand Award. His 1998 book, *Brandish,* and his 1999 book, *Deadwood,* were finalists for the Spur Award given by the Western Writers of America. He spent eight years as a mentor for the Jerry Jenkins Christian Writers Guild.

A short-story writer and the author of nearly forty books, Doug makes his home in Colorado Springs with his wife Kathy. They have two children, Rebecca and Derick. When not writing or traveling to research his novels, Doug enjoys restoring old English sports cars.